Gifted

Danielle Gillen

ISBN: 1543285430
ISBN-13: 978-1543285437

DEDICATION

For Heidi V.

CONTENTS

ACKNOWLEDGMENTS

Thank you to my beta readers, Pam Harris and Nancy Gillen. Thank you to Amy Shook for her careful proofreading. Much thanks to Markie Madden for the beautiful cover. Like all of my writing projects, this book started as a NaNo project, Camp NaNoWriMo to be exact. Thank you to NaNoWriMo for providing so much encouragement to so many writers. Good morning and thank you to Ramona DeFelice Long and the Writing Champions; much of this book was revised during the morning sprints. Thank you to the Heidis because I probably wouldn't write dog books without the Heidis. (And really, who wants to read books without dogs?) Thank you to Dad for starting the Heidis.

CHAPTER ONE

Frankie adjusted her blue scarf over her head, hiding her dark hair from view. She loved to walk and explore Superion City, but it was so much easier to explore when people thought she was just another city girl and didn't know her true identity. The southern edge of the city was her favorite. Away from the hustle and bustle, things were a little quieter here, but more importantly, people raised animals here on their little farms. Frankie loved animals, but she had never had a pet. Her parents wouldn't allow it.

There he was, the man who bred the dogs. Frankie knew the female dog had a litter two months ago. The pups were just now old enough to leave her, so the man had put them up for sale. Frankie had so wanted to buy one but had resisted. Her parents would only make her take it back anyway. Frankie watched as the man put a small black puppy into a bucket of water. The puppy was so cute! The man must be giving the puppy a bath before he went off to live with the lucky family who had bought him.

Frankie knew she must look nosy loitering around on the road. A farmer was bound to yell at her to move along. Until then, she would spy on the puppy. She couldn't wait to see the puppy after his bath. What would he think about it? Frankie waited, but something didn't seem right. The man didn't seem to be bathing the puppy so much as holding him under the water. The puppy was thrashing. She heard him yelp.

"Stop it! You're hurting him!" Frankie yelled. She ran toward them. So much for keeping a low profile on her walk.

"Go away, stupid girl," the man said. There was a farmer yelling at her. "I should have had the sense to drown him earlier. No one wants the scrawny runt, and I can't afford another mouth to feed."

Frankie couldn't help herself. She couldn't let this puppy die. "I will take him."

The man looked at Frankie as if she were crazy but thrust the puppy at her. Frankie hugged the sopping wet puppy to her chest. The puppy trembled, but he snuggled into the front of her dress. He seemed to already know he had found a friend in Frankie.

"How much?" Frankie asked.

"What?"

"I can pay you for him. How much?"

"I don't want your money. You're the only one dumb enough to buy a dog like that. Go away."

Frankie sure wasn't going to let the mean old man have another chance to hurt this puppy. She took off running, hugging the puppy tight. "Thank you!" she called over her shoulder.

Frankie kept running through the city. Most of the shops and businesses were closing for the day, and the winding streets were filling up with cars. Frankie dodged pedestrians on the sidewalks. She knew it wasn't ladylike to run, but oh well, running was faster than walking. She was grateful for her flat shoes. At least she had avoided those high heels that Mena tried to get her to wear. Frankie kept insisting she was too young and clumsy for high heels. Mena kept insisting Frankie needed to dress fancy. It was an endless battle. In any case, Mena wasn't going to be happy; she hated when Frankie was late. Frankie tucked the puppy in her bag as she ran. She only zipped it up halfway. The puppy would need to breathe in there. He would be safe and cozy until she could think of a way to explain him to Mena.

I have to get home! I have to get home! Frankie thought as loudly as she could in case any Minders were eavesdropping. It was only natural to think of the Minders when you had done something you weren't supposed to.

Frankie ducked as a brick flew by. "Sorry!" someone called. It must be a Reacher. They were constantly building things and tearing them down. As talented as they were at construction, they weren't careful. Innocent pedestrians always had to watch out for flying bricks and other debris.

Finally, she reached the northern edge of the city. Her legs burned as she ran up the long driveway to Superion Castle. The enormous stone castle was mysterious to most people, but to Frankie, it was just home. A guard held the door for her. She gave him a hurried wave as she ran past. If she stood still, the guard might notice that her bag was moving. She was so warm from running that she barely noticed the air conditioning that blasted through the castle. She kept running until she got to her room.

"Oh, thank goodness you're back, Princess Frances," Mena said with a sigh of relief as Frankie burst through the door. "I thought I was going to have to send out a search party."

"How many times do I have to ask you to call me Frankie? And I'm not that late." Frankie set her bag down carefully in the corner and hoped it was time for the puppy to take a nap.

"No, you're not that late, but according to Helen, lateness is certainly a habit of yours. You were probably getting into mischief too. Such behavior is not at all proper for a princess." Mena tried to look stern, but she mostly looked embarrassed.

Mena had only been Frankie's maid for a few weeks, and she wasn't used to correcting the princess. Helen, Frankie's former maid, had been a pro at it. Helen had recently retired, probably because she was tired of always correcting Frankie. Mena was only a couple years older than Frankie. Frankie knew this because she had asked Mena how old she was. She knew it was rude to ask adults their age, but Mena just looked so young. Mena was nineteen.

"I'm sorry. I'll try to be better," Frankie said. She didn't like to make Mena uncomfortable.

Mena stared at Frankie in horror. "Your dress! It's all wet and muddy. What did you do? You can't go on television like that."

Frankie looked down and inspected herself. A white dress was kind of asking to get dirty. She tried to think of an excuse, but it didn't matter as Mena didn't look like she had time to listen. She hustled Frankie into a clean dress and combed her hair.

Mena set down the comb and gave Frankie one last critical look. "Much better. Come on. Let's not keep your parents waiting."

Frankie hated to be involved with mandatory viewing, but she held her tongue. Mena escorted her through the castle's corridors. The walls were decorated with paintings, portraits of the former kings and queens of Superion. Frankie used to study the portraits when she was younger, so curious about the people who had lived so long ago. She didn't pay much attention to the portraits lately, but at least they brought some color to the otherwise gray castle.

When Frankie reached the quarters of King Leopold and Queen

Veronica, a guard let her in, and she was seated on a deep purple sofa between her parents. She resembled her mother. They had the same dark hair and slender frame. Queen Veronica was very beautiful. She had worked as a model when she was younger. King Leopold was blond and burly. He tended to intimidate people, Frankie included.

Mandatory viewing was exactly what it sounded like. There was an address, usually from the castle, and everyone in Superion was required to watch. This was a challenge for some. Not everyone had a television at home. Mandatory viewing didn't happen too frequently, only on holidays or when something big was happening in the kingdom. Tomorrow was big. It was the Test.

Queen Veronica set down the script she had been memorizing, and a red light blazed to life on the camera. They were live. Frankie smiled as pleasantly as she could. It was what she was expected to do.

"Good evening, Superion," Queen Veronica said. "It is the eve of an extremely important day in our kingdom. Another class of fourteen-year-olds will be taking the Test. As we all know, the Test results will determine the course of these young people's lives."

"The Test is exciting every year, but our family finds it especially thrilling this year," King Leopold said. "Our daughter, Frances, will be taking the Test. We can't wait to see what her Gift will be. We look forward to sharing her Gift with the kingdom."

"Good luck to all of our young Test-takers tomorrow. Good night, Superion," Queen Veronica said.

The camera switched off, and Frankie relaxed her face. Smiling like that made her cheeks hurt. The address had been brief, but she wished her parents didn't have to put her on television in front of the whole kingdom like a puppet, especially with the Test tomorrow. She had been able to set aside her anxiety about the Test during her adventure in the city, but now it was back in full force.

"Will I be eating dinner with you?" Frankie asked as she fiddled with the silver bracelet on her wrist. Frankie wasn't into jewelry, but she always wore it. Apparently, princesses were supposed to accessorize. Luckily for Frankie, Mena had an eye for accessorizing.

Frankie also wasn't into dining with her parents. Fortunately, that wasn't something she was required to do often. Her parents always talked forever about things that were going on in the kingdom, and Frankie was expected to sit and eat in silence. She was considered too young to understand anything that happened in the kingdom and too young to have any thoughts worth listening to.

"No, your father and I are much too busy for that," Queen Veronica said. "You will eat in your room with Mena tonight, but you will join us for breakfast tomorrow before the Test."

Frankie escorted herself back to her room. She was trusted to make her way back through the familiar corridors without getting into trouble. Geez, the castle was freezing! The air conditioning cut right through Frankie's thin summer dress. She walked faster.

"You were great!" Mena said as soon as Frankie walked in.

"Thanks, but I just sat there. It's hard to mess that up," Frankie said.

"I watched it on your television. I hope you don't mind. It was mandatory, so I figured it would be okay."

"You can watch that television whenever you want." Frankie rarely watched television, so Mena might as well enjoy it. Between news reports on the actual royals and fictional stories about royals, almost everything on television was about royals. Royals lost their mystique when you were one.

Mena didn't sit down until after Frankie had. Frankie immediately dug into her supper of vegetable lasagna. She was starving. Mena never took a break. She sat down across from Frankie to work on some knitting.

"Why don't you eat?" Frankie asked.

"You know I eat in the servants' quarters, Princess. It wouldn't be proper for me to dine with my mistress."

Frankie swallowed a bite of lasagna. It was delicious. "I think that's silly. You must be hungry. Why are there so many rules anyway?"

"I don't know. That's just the way it is, especially here in Superion. Your mother and father like things to be very proper."

Frankie had expected such an answer. Over the years, she had received many lectures on what was proper. Most of those lectures had been delivered by Helen. Frankie knew rules were important, but did there have to be so many? She decided now wasn't the time to push the issue. Mena probably didn't know any better than she did. Instead, she ate quietly.

"Pardon me if this is too bold, but are you nervous about the Test?" Mena said.

"Yes." It was the first time Frankie had admitted it out loud. Was it okay to be nervous? Was it okay to admit it?

All Frankie knew about the Test was this: You took the Test when you finished primary school. Your Test result determined where you went to secondary school, and the rest of your life. Your Test result was either you were Gifted or you were not. A Gift was something you were born with, and the Test determined if it was there. You couldn't study or prepare for the Test. No one told the kids what it was like, and it likely changed over time.

"I was nervous too. I think everyone is," Mena said.

"Was it awful? Were you disappointed to find out you were Not Gifted?" All of the servants were Not Gifted. Some of the Not Gifted begrudged the Gifted and were bitter, but Frankie didn't sense any of that from Mena.

"Not at all. Not everyone can be Gifted. Besides, I don't think I have done too badly in life. Not too many people get to spend every day in a castle. I don't think you have anything to worry about though. Nearly all royals are Gifted."

Frankie looked down at her empty plate. Maybe she should have saved some lasagna for the puppy. Did puppies like lasagna? She glanced over at her bag in the corner. The puppy was quiet in there. He must still be napping. Frankie had some cookies stashed away. She could feed him cookies after Mena went to bed. Everyone liked cookies. She would have to figure out a way to get him proper dog food though. She doubted an all-cookie diet was good for puppies.

Mena set down her knitting. "I'll go start your shower. A shower and then bed. You have a big day tomorrow."

CHAPTER TWO

Frankie stepped into the shower. It was the exact perfect temperature. All Mena had to do was push a button for her, and it was perfect. Then when she needed shampoo and soap, Frankie pushed more buttons. It was one of the privileges of being a royal. Some of the people of Superion enjoyed similar technology as the royals, mainly the Gifted. The Not Gifted were lucky to have any warm water at all.

As Frankie let the perfect temperature warm water rain down on her, she couldn't help but think about royalty and Gifts. With the Test less than twenty-four hours away, it was hard to think of anything else. What Mena had said about royals was true. If Frankie took after her family, she would certainly be Gifted. Then again, what if she was the exception? There had to be an exception somewhere, and what if she was the one royal who was Not Gifted?

If she hoped to be Gifted, Frankie didn't know which Gift she wished for. There were three types of Gifts.

First, there was the Gift of the Mind. Minders could read the thoughts of others around them. They could also project their thoughts to others, although other Minders were usually the only people who could understand. Minders made Frankie a little uncomfortable. It was a great Gift, but she wasn't sure she liked the idea of reading other people's thoughts. Minders often did life-saving things like stop criminals before they even had an opportunity to carry out their crimes, but shouldn't thoughts be private? Frankie didn't have many secrets, but that didn't mean she wanted someone to read her thoughts. The fact was, Minders probably read her thoughts every day, and she was completely oblivious. Now that she thought about it, Minders were a little creepy.

The next Gift was the Gift of Reach. Reachers could move objects without touching them. It would be nice to summon things when she wanted them, but was that really necessary? Her arms and legs worked perfectly well. If she wanted anything, she could get up and get it. Reachers could easily do things like construct buildings. It took a lot of control but didn't require any physical strength or equipment. It was another special Gift, but the Gift of the Reacher didn't appeal to Frankie much more than the Gift of the Minder did. She had never aspired to build things.

The third and final Gift was the Gift of Travel. This was the Gift that Frankie was the most familiar with as her parents were both Travelers. Travelers could will themselves anywhere they liked. Like the Reacher, the Gift of the Traveler required a lot of control. You had to really focus on where you wanted to go. Otherwise, you could wind up anywhere. Not all Travelers could take others with them when they Traveled, but the king and queen were very powerful with their Gift. They had taken Frankie all over Superion. Of course, their royal duties required them to Travel daily, and they only took her along once in a great while. Still, she had experienced what a significant Gift the Gift of Travel was. If she followed in her parents' footsteps as expected, she would learn that was her Gift tomorrow. That would be an honor, but Frankie didn't have any problem getting around with non-Gifted methods. She was content to walk or run. If she needed, she could always hire a car. Maybe she could even learn to drive a car when she got older.

Frankie decided she didn't have a wish for any particular Gift. Whatever her Gift, she would appreciate it. She would have to as the course of her life would depend on it. She didn't think Not Gifted would be that bad either though. Mena seemed happy enough. Frankie could always get a job like Mena's. Frankie didn't know much about cooking and cleaning, but if that was her fate, she could learn. If she could learn to harness a Gift if she had to, she could learn to cook and clean.

Resolving herself to the fact that she would have to deal with whatever her Test result turned out to be, Frankie also decided she was clean enough and had probably used up enough of the perfectly warm water. After pushing the button to turn off the water, she dried herself in a plush towel and dressed in her most favorite, softest pajamas. They were one of her favorite parts of being a princess. She had no interest in elegant gowns. Soft pajamas were the best. If she ended up Not Gifted and poor, Frankie would save up her money to buy soft pajamas.

Frankie sat still as Mena blow dried and brushed her long hair. Mena didn't trust Frankie to take care of her own hair. She had good reason. When left to her own devices, Frankie went to bed with her hair wet, which resulted in an endless mess of tangles in the morning. Mena was patient, but she preferred to prevent Frankie's tangles if she could. Frankie thought short hair would be more practical. She had given herself a haircut once. She had gotten a pair of scissors and chopped her hair to her shoulder. It had been a good idea. It would be much easier to care for, but it wasn't too short. She still looked like a girl. Helen had been mortified, and the queen had been furious. Everyone except Frankie seemed to think that princesses should have long hair. Frankie never tried to give herself a haircut again.

Frankie didn't mind Mena taking care of her hair too much. It was relaxing in a way. She had to sit quietly though. She and Mena often found little things to chat about through the day, but the blow dryer would drown out any attempt at conversation. But Frankie heard a noise other than the roar of the blow dryer tonight. She wondered if Mena could hear it. The puppy must have had a long enough nap. Frankie would have to share her secret with Mena eventually, but she wasn't sure how to do so and was hoping to wait until tomorrow at least. The noise kept going, and it was getting louder.

Mena switched off the blow dryer. "There, all finished. Would you like me to get your hot cocoa?"

"Yes, thank you," Frankie said. As much as she loved hot cocoa, she was even more anxious to get Mena out of the room.

Mena was almost to the door when Frankie's bag jumped. She froze.

"Princess Frances? Did you see that?"

"Um, it's okay." Frankie wasn't sure what else to say.

"Okay? I think there's a rat in your bag. You know I hate rats." Mena was losing her usual calm demeanor.

"It's not a rat. It's something much more pleasant. Just don't panic." There was no delaying it now. Frankie crossed the room and took the puppy out of her bag. He was very happy to see her after his nap. He wagged his tail and licked her face.

Mena gasped. "A puppy?"

"Yes. See, he's much nicer than a rat." Frankie set the puppy on the floor and sat down next to him.

"Your parents don't know about this, do they? You know they hate animals. Helen told me you could be a handful, but I had hoped you were growing out of that."

"They don't know. Please don't tell them. I so want to keep him. I have to keep him. He can be our secret," Frankie begged.

The puppy had made his way over to Mena. He sniffed the hem of her dress with great curiosity. Mena looked like she was trying not to smile. "Well, I suppose it could work. Your parents never come to your room. If we keep him here, they needn't know." She bent down and tentatively pet the puppy's head. He licked her fingers in return. "Letting him out to do his business may be a challenge."

Mena was being won over! Frankie knew she would be. The puppy was too cute not to love. She was also glad her parents weren't Minders. If they were, she would never get away with this.

"Actually, I think he has to go out now," Frankie said.

"Really? What makes you say that? How do you know?"

"I don't know." It was strange. Frankie didn't know how she knew. She just did.

"Okay. I'll take him. I'll go down to the kitchen to get your hot cocoa, and I'll sneak out the kitchen door with him for a few minutes. It's dark out, and we'll be quick." Mena scooped up the puppy. "I don't think anyone will notice us. I'll need to borrow your bag." Mena put the squirming puppy in the bag and slipped it over her shoulder. "We shall return."

Frankie sat anxiously. She hoped Mena wouldn't get caught. She also hoped Mena wouldn't change her mind on the puppy. The poor puppy had been through an ordeal already. Frankie had to keep him. Sitting wasn't doing any good. She stood and started to pace.

Frankie caught a glimpse of her reflection in the mirror as she paced. She guessed her hair did look nice after Mena had spent so much time with it. Her dark hair hung almost to her waist. She knew her dark hair dramatically offset her light eyes. She also knew some of the kids in primary school thought she was pretty. It was flattering, but it was sad when people only liked you because you were pretty and a princess. None of the kids at school had really wanted to be her friend. They had no interest in adventuring around the city like Frankie liked to do. Instead, they just wanted to see the castle and meet the king and queen. Frankie could see why they thought that was exciting, but after they had seen the castle and all of its fancy things, they quickly lost interest in Frankie. That made Frankie a loner. At least she had Mena. Her maid could also be her friend, right? She also now had a puppy for a friend. Frankie looked out the window. Were they still outside? It was too dark to tell.

There were footsteps out in the hall. Frankie sat back down and tried to look calm. What if her mother or father had decided to pay her a surprise visit? It was unlikely, but what if her mother or father were here when Mena came back? That would ruin everything. She let out a sigh of relief when the door opened and Mena entered.

"We made it," a flushed Mena said. She had a bag on each shoulder and a tray with hot cocoa in her hand. After locking the door securely behind her, she unloaded her goods. The puppy burst out of one bag, and Mena took food out of the other.

"I thought this little guy might be hungry, so I took some scraps from the kitchen," Mena said. She set some food and water in bowls on the floor. The puppy started eating immediately.

"He was starving," Frankie said. She knew this. It was logical. She doubted the mean old man had fed him that much, and the puppy was sure happy to eat now. It was something more than that though. Like she had known he had to go out, she knew he had been hungry.

Frankie sipped her hot cocoa as she watched the puppy eat. Hot cocoa was her absolute favorite treat, even when it was summer like it was now. Her father liked cold and kept the castle overly air conditioned, so Frankie was always looking for a way to warm up. She was tempted to light a fire in the fireplace, but if she did, her father would be furious.

Mena sat down across from Frankie. "So, did you come up with a name for him yet?"

"I was thinking Zac. What do you think?"

Mena nodded. "Zac is a nice name."

Frankie reached down and rubbed the puppy's head. "I will call you Zac," she stated, making it official. Zac licked her fingers as if to say he approved.

"Now Frankie, I like Zac and want you to keep him, but you have to be honest with me. How did you get him? You didn't do anything illegal, did you?" Mena looked very serious.

"No, I didn't do anything illegal. I don't know what Helen told you about me, but she clearly exaggerated." Frankie went on to tell Mena how she had taken Zac from the mean old man.

"You saved Zac's life. You had to do it," Mena said. "I can't believe someone wanted to kill an innocent puppy. Some people are so cruel."

Zac had found one of Frankie's teddy bears and played with it. His sharp puppy teeth may tear the fabric, but Frankie didn't mind. She was getting a little old for teddy bears anyway. Zac wagged his tail as he played. He was delighted with his new toy. The girls watched him play for a while. Eventually, he flopped down with a big yawn.

"It looks like someone is ready for bed," Mena said. She picked up the sleepy puppy and tucked him into Frankie's bed. "It's bedtime for all of us. Princess Frances needs a good night's sleep before her big Test, and puppies need sleep to grow, and I am just tired."

** ** **

Zac couldn't believe the bed. It was so soft! He didn't know anything could be this soft. There had been blankets at his old house, but those had been scratchy and not soft at all. This bed was like sleeping on a cloud! He cuddled close to the girl. She was already asleep. She was a princess! A princess had rescued him from the mean old man! She was very brave, and she was Zac's hero. He had almost died today, but what a turn his little puppy life had taken. He had to be the luckiest puppy in the kingdom.

I love you, Princess, he thought as he dozed off.

CHAPTER THREE

Frankie awoke to Zac licking her face. It tickled. "Good morning, Zac."

"Good morning, Princess Frances," Mena called from the corner of the room. She was busy selecting an outfit from Frankie's wardrobe. It looked like Frankie wouldn't be allowed to wear pajamas all day.

"My name is Frankie," Frankie told Zac. "Mena is difficult."

Frankie would have been content to play with Zac, but that wasn't to be. Today was the Test. She was so nervous! If she pretended to be sick, would she be allowed to stay home? Probably not. The Test was such a big deal that it was probably against the law to miss it. Frankie pushed the cozy blankets away and reluctantly got out of bed.

Mena ushered Frankie about, dressing her up like a doll. Frankie wore one of her prettiest dresses. It was a dusty pink with silver embroidery. Mena paired it with silver bracelets and silver high heels. Frankie hated wearing high heels. She always felt like she was going to fall. Mena styled Frankie's dark hair perfectly and even painted her face with makeup. Evidently Frankie wasn't too young for makeup anymore.

"I know the Test is a big deal, but is all of this really necessary?" Frankie griped.

"Not for the other girls, but it is for you," Mena said. "You're the princess, so all eyes will be on you. You have to look extra nice."

After Mena was finally finished and deemed Frankie's appearance acceptable, it was time to go. Frankie rubbed Zac's soft fur. "I will see you later," she promised. "I think he likes me," she told Mena.

Frankie took her seat in the formal dining room. She was grateful she didn't have to join her parents for meals often, but she did like the dining room. It made her wonder about the feasts that had occurred here many years ago. Her parents hadn't continued the tradition of hosting feasts. While they allowed Frankie to have a classmate visit now and then, as a rule, they didn't want outsiders in the castle.

When her meal was set in front of her, Frankie tried not to make a face. She ended up mostly pushing the food around the plate. Her favorite breakfast was oatmeal. Mena prepared it for her every day. This breakfast was disgusting. It was mostly sausage and bacon, which Frankie didn't care for. She liked animals. She didn't like to eat them. Mena honored this wish. Her parents thought it was silly and childish. Maybe Mena thought it was silly too but wanted to give Frankie food she would eat. There were a few strawberries on the plate seemingly for decoration; Frankie ate those.

Frankie couldn't see why her parents had insisted they all have breakfast together this morning. So far, they had barely acknowledged her. As usual, they were discussing the kingdom as if she wasn't even there.

"These Not Gifted are getting out of hand," King Leopold was saying.

"Oh yes," Queen Veronica said. "They want much more than they are due. Thinking they deserve the same wages as the Gifted. That is ridiculous!"

"I don't know what they are thinking," King Leopold said. "They're not equal to the Gifted, and that's their own fault."

Frankie didn't agree with this at all. A Gift was something you were born with, not a choice, so it was wrong to blame someone for being Not Gifted. Plus, maybe some of the Not Gifted did deserve higher wages. Look at Mena. She was Not Gifted, and she worked extremely hard. Frankie didn't say any of this out loud. Her parents seemed to think her a very bad child if she had any opinions, especially if those opinions were different from their own.

"Are you excited for your Test?" Queen Veronica asked Frankie, as if just noticing she was there.

Frankie shrugged. Excited was definitely not the word she would choose.

"We will have to sort out your arrangements for secondary school, but I suppose we can do that later," King Leopold said.

"I haven't even taken my Test yet," Frankie protested. She stared down at the table.

"Nonsense. The Test is just a formality," King Leopold said. "We know you're going to be a Traveler. How could you possibly be anything else? The real question is what to do about your education. The Travelers School is excellent, or we could get you a private tutor. I guess we will see."

"You will love Traveling," Queen Veronica said. "Oh, I can't wait to tell everyone about the Traveling Princess."

Frankie studied the table's wood grain as she tried not to panic. Even though Mena had told her everyone was nervous about the Test, that hadn't made her feel any better. Now her parents' enthusiasm was making her even more nervous. She was expected to be a Traveler, but what if she wasn't?

The Test was given in the primary school. Frankie sat in her usual classroom at her usual metal desk. The kids took the Test one at a time. When it was her turn, Frankie would be called into the next room to finally take the Test. They were going in alphabetical order. With the last name Westwood, Frankie would be one of the last ones. She watched the classroom slowly empty around her. She tried to think of something – anything – other than her impending Test, but it wasn't working.

Frankie wished she knew what the Test was like. It most likely involved answering questions. That was what all of the tests were like. If that was the case, she hoped it was multiple choice. She didn't even want to think about writing an essay on a Test she wasn't able to prepare for. On the other hand, what if the Test was some sort of exercise like in gym class? The girls wouldn't do too well with that. They were only allowed to stand and cheer for the boys in gym class. Girls weren't encouraged to be athletic in Superion. Frankie would have an advantage over some of the girls in that case. At least she liked to adventure and run in her free time.

After what felt like years, Frankie's name was called, and she went into the Testing room.

"Hello," the Test Administrator said. Frankie didn't recognize him. He wasn't one of the teachers at the school. He looked to be a little bit older than Mena, and he wore a white coat.

"Hi," Frankie managed to say quietly.

"It is lovely to meet you, Princess Frances," he said. "Please have a seat."

Frankie silently sat in the only chair in the room. She knew she should try to act more sociable and more like a princess, but she was too puzzled by this Test. She only had a chair. No desk. No pencil or paper. This was definitely not a written Test.

"Roll up your sleeve please," he said.

Even more puzzled, Frankie did as she was instructed.

"Don't be frightened. This will be quick," he said. He smiled, which Frankie guessed was supposed to be reassuring.

He rubbed something over her arm. Then he pricked her with something that drew blood out. It hurt, but Frankie forced herself to be brave. She resisted the urge to cry or try to escape.

"There. That wasn't so bad, was it?" The man bandaged her arm. Then he turned his attention to some instruments on a table and seemed to forget about Frankie entirely.

Frankie stared down at her white bandage. Did it go with her outfit? She didn't know. She wasn't good at such things. "That was it? That was the Test? All you do is take my blood?" That seemed too simple.

"Take your blood and then read it," he corrected. "You have heard that a Gift is something you are born with, right?"

Frankie looked up and nodded.

"These instruments allow us to read your blood. Each Gift is a different anomaly in the blood, so that's what I'm looking for here."

"What do you see in mine?" Frankie asked anxiously.

"That is very interesting indeed."

Frankie was then led into the principal's office. She wasn't in trouble, but that was where they were reading the Test results. Apparently most parents thought the principal's office was more comfortable than a classroom. The Test results were always given with the parents present. Frankie's parents were already there and waiting. They were on the edge of their seats with excitement. Frankie took her place in the chair between them. She had to admit she was starting to feel a little excited herself, now that the Test itself was over.

"King Leopold, Queen Veronica, it is an honor," the Test Administrator said with a bow. "Thank you for entrusting me to test Princess Frances."

King Leopold brushed this off. He usually appreciated when the citizens of Superion showed their respect, but today he wasn't interested. "Well, let's hear the results," he said.

The Test Administrator sat in the chair that was usually the principal's. The princess's Test results were very surprising – "

"Of course! She is probably the most powerful Traveler ever tested," King Leopold interrupted, beaming.

"No, that's not it," the Test Administrator said. "The princess is not a Traveler."

King Leopold's face was turning a furious red. "What do you mean, not a Traveler? She must be a Traveler! There must be some mistake!"

"It's okay if you're not a Traveler, Frankie," Queen Veronica said unconvincingly. "What is her Gift then? Is she a Minder? Is she a Reacher? Those are both respectable Gifts." She looked at the Test Administrator hopefully.

"The princess is indeed Gifted, but I cannot tell you what her Gift is," the Test Administrator said. He spoke quickly so as not to be interrupted again. "Her blood patterns do not match that for Not Gifted, so that can be ruled out. However, the patterns do not fit with Travelers, Minders, or Reachers. She is very unique. Whatever her Gift is, it must be very special."

"That is a lie! You must have made a mistake! No one gets an inconclusive Test result," King Leopold said. His face was going from red to purple. "Come on, Frankie. Let's go."

Frankie hustled out of the school and into the car. There was a crowd of photographers and reporters. They frantically took Frankie's picture and shouted questions, desperate to know what her Gift was. Frankie didn't respond, nor did her parents. There had probably been an address planned for today, but Frankie doubted it would happen now. Today had not gone according to plan.

** ** **

Zac played with his teddy bear. It was fun. There hadn't been toys at his old house. He missed the princess. He hoped she would be back soon. The other girl, Mena, was here. She bustled about the rooms, straightening up. Mena was nice. She had found food for Zac a few times now.

"Come on, Zac. You must have to do your business again," Mena said.

Zac. That was his name. None of the puppies had been given names at his old house.

Mena lifted him up and put him in the bag again. Zac didn't know why he had to be carried around in the bag. His paws worked. He could walk. It was hot and stuffy in the bag. He started to squirm.

"Shh, you have to be still in there, or we'll get caught. Okay?" Mena said.

Zac wished he could see where they were going, but he obediently tried to be as still as he could. Finally, Mena let him out. They were in the grass. She had brought him here a few times already. He was expected to go potty here. Now that he thought about it, he did have to go. He couldn't stray too far from Mena. She had attached a rope to his neck. He wore one end, and she held the other. He went potty up against the wall.

"Good boy," Mena said.

"Mena, are you out here?" a man's voice called.

"Oh no," Mena whispered. She scooped Zac up as fast as she could and shoved him into the bag.

"Yes, I'm here," Mena called, slightly breathless.

"What are you doing out here?" the man asked.

Zac didn't like this man. He couldn't see this man, and he had probably never met this man before. This man seemed mean though, like the mean old man who had tried to kill him.

"I was gathering flowers for Princess Frances," Mena said. "I thought it would be a nice surprise for her. She has had a big day with her Test. Excuse me. I need to get back upstairs."

They were on the move again, quickly this time. A minute later they were climbing the stairs.

That was close, Mena, Zac thought.

** ** **

Frankie pet Zac's head sleepily. He had been so happy to see her when she came home. Now he was sound asleep in her lap. Frankie knew that he was still a puppy and that he would grow, but if possible, he already looked bigger than yesterday. Another change from yesterday was the blue fabric collar around his neck. Mena had made it today.

"I like his collar," Frankie said.

"I'm glad, Princess," Mena said.

Frankie and Mena sat at the small table in Frankie's room. Frankie slowly sipped her hot cocoa. It felt good to be back in her room with Zac and Mena. She had eaten supper with the king and queen. Instead of discussing Superion as they usually did, her parents had spent the meal discussing her future. Frankie found the whole thing quite distressing.

"I found a leash too," Mena said. "It's nothing fancy, just some rope, but it will do until I can make him a nicer one. Every pet should have a leash and a collar. Besides, I can't have him getting too curious when we're outside. He could run off and get lost, and that wouldn't be good at all." Mena's hands flew at her knitting as she spoke.

"Good idea," Frankie said. "The flowers are pretty too." Mena had picked flowers today, and they brought a bit of summer to Frankie's always cold room. Mena had been a busy lady today.

"I'm glad you like them," Mena said. "Now, are you going to tell me your big news, or should I listen to the staff gossip to find out? What was your Test result?"

"They couldn't tell me," Frankie mumbled into her mug.

"What do you mean they couldn't tell you?" Mena said. She set down her yarn. "Did they have a problem drawing the blood? I heard that can happen sometimes."

"No, they took my blood, but they couldn't tell me what my Test result was. They say I'm Gifted, but I'm not a Minder, Reacher, or Traveler."

"What other Gift is there?" Mena said.

"I don't know. There probably isn't one. My blood is probably some abnormal version of Not Gifted." Frankie still didn't think being Not Gifted would be that bad a fate. If her Test result had been Not Gifted, she would at least know her fate. All of her classmates had taken the Test today, and they were all celebrating or lamenting their results right now. Frankie was the only one still wondering.

"I don't think that's true at all," Mena said. "I bet you have an extremely special Gift. You'll see."

Frankie knew Mena was trying to cheer her up, but she didn't think it was working. She kept petting Zac. She had been so anxious before the Test. Now the Test was over, and she was still anxious. Gifted or not, she wanted to know what she was. She didn't know how or when she would find that out.

"I guess this complicates the matter of secondary school," Mena said. "What are you going to do?"

Frankie shrugged. "My parents haven't decided yet." They had been discussing it nonstop since hearing the results, and they seemed to be favoring sending Frankie to the Travelers School. Frankie didn't think that was a good idea if she wasn't a Traveler, but she also didn't think she had a say in the matter.

"Oh well. Try not to worry about it too much," Mena said. "School doesn't start up for a few weeks anyway. You can enjoy some summer vacation in the meantime."

That was true. Frankie had been so caught up in the Test that she hadn't even thought of summer vacation. She loved summer!

"I think I'll take Zac on an adventure tomorrow," she decided. "I bet he'll like that."

"Yes, he probably will, but do be careful, Princess Frances," Mena said.

"You don't need to call me Princess Frances," Frankie said for what seemed like the millionth time. "Helen never did." She set down her now empty mug.

"Oh, all right, Frances."

"Frankie."

"Frankie sounds like a boy's name. I don't know what you have against your full name. Frances is a nice name."

"I could use my full name if I had a nice name like Mena, but I don't," Frankie said.

"My full name is not Mena," Mena admitted. "It's short for Filomena, and you will call me Mena."

CHAPTER FOUR

"Frankie, wake up!"

Frankie struggled to drag herself back from a deep sleep. She was in her warm soft bed. Zac jumped on her excitedly. Mena stood over her, looking flustered. Frankie racked her brain to try to remember why she was being woken up. Did she have to go to school? Did she have to take the Test? No, she had done those things already.

"I thought it was summer vacation," she finally said.

"So did I," Mena said.

"Then why do I have to get up? I get to sleep in on summer vacation," Frankie whined.

"I don't know why you have to get up, but you do," Mena said, pulling the cozy lavender blankets away. "Your parents want you dressed and downstairs immediately. Come on."

A few minutes later Frankie was in the formal dining room. She was allowed to wear one of her simple dresses, and her hair was pulled back. She was glad she didn't have to wear the formal dress, but in the rush, there hadn't been time for breakfast. She was starving. She glanced around the room, hoping for a bit of fruit, but there was no food in sight. Whatever she had to be here for, it wasn't breakfast.

"Oh good, you're finally here," Queen Veronica said. "Are you ready?"

"Ready for what?" Frankie said. She was still waiting for someone to fill her in.

"School," Queen Veronica said. "The tutor your father and I had been considering gladly agreed to the job. You will start your lessons this morning. Isn't it exciting?"

Frankie wasn't excited. Disappointed was more like it. "But it's summer vacation. None of the other kids will be starting lessons yet."

"Don't be such a child," Queen Veronica snapped. "Royals do not get vacations. There is always work to be done, and you have to learn to work harder. If you're not careful, you will end up lazy like those Not Gifted. That is not at all proper for a princess. Ah, here he is."

King Leopold led a man into the room. Frankie had never had a male teacher before. All of her teachers at the primary school had been female. The tutor had short gray hair and bright blue eyes. He was dressed in a neat suit and looked quite serious.

"Princess Frances," he said, inclining his head. He didn't bow. She was only a princess, not a queen.

"Frankie, this is Mr. Thomas Tate, your tutor," King Leopold said. "Your mother and I had hoped to observe your first lesson, but we must be off. You are in good hands." With a nod, he and Queen Veronica used their Gift to leave. The king and queen's Traveling was impressive to most, but Frankie was used to it.

"Would you look at that?" Mr. Tate said, delighted. "Your parents are clearly very Gifted. It takes a lot of skill to Travel on a whim like that. Most Travelers need to concentrate on where they are going, sometimes for a long time, before they can leave. Your parents seem to barely need to give it a thought. How about that? I bet you will be able to do that soon too."

"Didn't they tell you my Test results?" Frankie said anxiously.

"Yes, your father did mention they were abnormal," Mr. Tate said. "However, your father and I are in agreement. Given your family, you are most likely a Traveler, so I will train you as one. There is an outside chance that you could be a Minder or a Reacher. I know the principles of their training, so we will work on that a bit too. We'll see what sticks. Does that sound like a plan?"

Frankie nodded. The plan made sense, but it also sounded like a big waste of time. It would be logical training if she possessed one of those three Gifts, but according to the Test, she did not. She also thought her parents were a little delusional to be so eager for her to undergo the Traveler training when her Test said she was not a Traveler.

"Good then. Let's get to it, Princess Frances," Mr. Tate said. He clapped his hands with enthusiasm.

"You can call me Frankie," she offered. All of her teachers at the primary school had called her Frankie eventually.

"In that case, you may as well call me Thomas," he said. "This morning will be Traveler training since that is the obvious place to start."

Frankie tried to smile pleasantly, but she didn't think it came out right. The dining room was serving as their classroom. She was instructed to stand on one side of the room and think about her destination, the other side of the room.

"Breathe and focus," Thomas instructed. "Don't let yourself get upset. Just stay calm and focus on your destination."

Frankie planted her feet and focused. This exercise must be a standard one for beginner Traveler training. Everyone must start small. If they tried going too far too fast, they could end up getting lost, and that would be dangerous. At the same time, her destination was the other side of the room. Why couldn't she walk there? Walking was the only way she would ever get across a room. She knew she didn't possess the Gift of Travel.

She decided to play along with the lesson anyway. There was nothing else for it. She focused and focused. To her surprise, she moved forward the tiniest bit. She was still not to her destination, but she had Traveled. She had really Traveled. Then Thomas said no. He had seen her step forward. She had not really Traveled.

Frankie went back to focusing. She focused on her destination, but she also focused on her feet. Evidently they wanted to move, but that was cheating. She tried not to focus on her stomach, which was very much craving food.

Yesterday morning had felt long. Time had passed slowly while she had waited for her turn to take the Test. This morning felt like an eternity. She kept focusing on the dining room even though the dining room was turning into the last place she wanted to be.

Thomas tried to be encouraging. He kept telling her "Breathe and see yourself at your destination" and "Relax and let your Gift do the work." Frankie knew he meant well, but she was getting frustrated. She focused and resisted the urge to run from the room.

Finally, Mena brought them a reprieve when she entered the dining room with a tray of food.

"I'm sorry to interrupt," Mena said. "I thought the two of you might want a lunch break. You must be working hard in here."

Thomas looked puzzled by this idea. "Yes, I suppose we should take a break," he said after a moment.

Frankie was so relieved she could have hugged them both. She gratefully joined Thomas at the table. Her legs were stiff as she walked; she had been standing still for too long. Her plate was piled high with a variety of cheeses, vegetables, and bread. It looked delicious. It was more than she usually ate for lunch, but Mena must have realized she hadn't eaten breakfast and would be especially hungry. Mena was so smart.

Frankie thought it was a little strange that she would be eating with her teacher. Students and teachers had never eaten together at the primary school. Eating together must have been normal to Thomas. He didn't pay much attention to Frankie. Instead, he read a book. Frankie was glad he didn't expect her to keep up a conversation. She had no idea what you talked about with a teacher.

If princesses were supposed to be dainty and not eat too much, Frankie failed. She ate every bite of her lunch. Mena had even included a bit of chocolate as a treat. Mena knew how much Frankie loved chocolate. After a morning that had felt like forever, Frankie had never needed chocolate more. She was disappointed when lunch was over. She had plenty to eat and was no longer hungry, but she didn't want to go back to the lesson.

Thomas set his book aside. "Back to work," he said.

Frankie stood and started to walk back to her corner. Like it or not, it looked like she would be focusing all afternoon.

"No, you can sit down. I think we worked on Traveler training enough for today," Thomas said.

Frankie couldn't agree more. She sat down as Thomas took heavy textbooks from his bag. By reading the spines, Frankie could see that they were math and language. These lessons she could do.

The afternoon flew by. The material was a little more difficult than primary school, but Frankie picked it up quickly. After a morning of failing at Traveling, it felt good to work on subjects she was good at. Thomas seemed a little surprised by Frankie.

"You're doing well with this," he said. "My students usually hate this part. They would rather work on their Gift all day long."

"I don't have a Gift yet," Frankie said as she worked out a math problem. "And I don't mind school. I would rather have summer vacation, but school isn't so bad."

Frankie and Thomas both jumped when the king and queen burst into the room at the end of the afternoon. They didn't come in through the door as most people would have. They used their Gift of Travel.

King Leopold eyed the textbooks with distaste. "What are you studying that for?"

"These subjects are as much a part of Frankie's education as the Gifts," Thomas said. "We agreed that it is best for Frankie, like all students, to have a well-rounded secondary education."

King Leopold looked like he didn't agree at all, but Queen Veronica jumped in. "Did you do the Traveler lesson today? How did it go?" she said.

"Yes, we did the Traveler lesson. It is not clear that Frankie is a Traveler," Thomas said carefully.

"She can't Travel? What do you mean?" King Leopold demanded. His face was turning angry red again. "You must be an incompetent Traveling instructor."

"She didn't Travel today. That doesn't mean she's not a Traveler. Even some of the most skilled Travelers have a tough go of it at first," Thomas said.

King Leopold didn't look entirely convinced.

"We'll keep working. Frankie is a bright girl. I'm sure everything will work out fantastically, no matter what her Gift will be," Thomas said.

The mention that Frankie's Gift was still unknown seemed to horrify the king and queen. Frankie was thankful that Thomas was open-minded about her Gift, even if this morning's Traveling lesson had felt like torture.

"Goodbye, Frankie. I will see you tomorrow," Thomas said with a wink.

"Goodbye. Thank you for my lesson," Frankie said. She felt like maybe Thomas was on her side.

** ** **

Zac was getting used to this. Mena would carry him in the bag for a few minutes. Then they were outside. She would put the leash on him, and he could roam a bit as long as he was quick. Zac was happy to be outside. As nice as the castle was, it felt good to be outside where there was fresh air and grass.

"Mena, there you are!" a man's voice called.

Mena gasped. "Zac, quick!" she whispered. She hurried Zac back into the bag. Zac would like to see the man's face. The voice was familiar, but he was also getting the idea that it was important for the girls to put him in this bag.

"Picking flowers again?" the man said.

"Yes," Mena said. "Princess Frances just loves wildflowers."

"What's in the bag?"

"Flowers."

"I don't believe you," he said. Zac was pulled forward as the bag was roughly torn from Mena's shoulder. The man opened the bag and looked down at Zac. Zac stared up at the man. He didn't like the man one bit. Zac couldn't help himself. He let out a growl.

"Mean little mutt," the man said, thrusting the bag away. "You know you can't keep him, Mena. The king and queen don't allow any pets. You really must be an ungrateful maid to sneak him into the castle. You'll be out of a job when the king and queen find out."

Mena grabbed the bag back and hugged it to her chest. Zac could feel her heart beating very fast. "Please, I must keep him. Please don't tell anyone," she begged.

"I don't know," the man said. He seemed to be enjoying Mena's distress. "I could keep a secret if you gave me some incentive. I could think of something."

"What?" Mena said. She sounded frightened.

"Go on a date with me. Tonight."

"You know I can't. I have to care for the princess."

"I don't mind late. I will meet you at eleven. It's that, or I tell everyone about your little secret."

** ** **

Frankie sat on the lavender rug in her bedroom and played with Zac and the teddy bear. She would give the teddy bear a little toss, and Zac would bring it back, wagging his tail a mile a minute. It was so much fun having a puppy. She couldn't understand why her parents hated animals.

"Here is your hot cocoa, Frankie. I brought some cookies for you and Zac to share as well," Mena said as she walked into the room. She set the tray on the table. "If you don't mind, I will be going. Good night."

"Good night," Frankie replied, puzzled. She knew she didn't need Mena to sit with her and tuck her in. She was getting a little old for those things anyway, but she was used to Mena's company. Frankie liked Mena's company. She wondered if anything was wrong. For a reason she couldn't explain, an image of the royal driver popped into her head.

CHAPTER FIVE

Mena knew most girls dressed up for dates, but she didn't bother. Fancy clothes weren't exactly something she owned anyway. She could have borrowed something from Frankie, but that would have been inappropriate. She wore her usual black dress, and her fair hair was tucked into its bun.

Mena walked into the garage and looked around suspiciously. Adam, the royal driver, gave her the creeps. He had a reputation for preying on the female help. Helen and all of the other women had warned her. She didn't want to go on this date. She knew it was a foolish thing to do, but she couldn't have the king and queen finding out about Zac. If the puppy was taken away, it would break Frankie's heart.

"Good evening. You look pretty tonight," Adam said.

"Hello," Mena said. She forced herself to smile. Even if she didn't want to be here, she could at least act pleasant and pretend.

Adam unlocked one of the cars. "Shall we?"

Mena toyed with the cuff of her long sleeve nervously. "I didn't think we were allowed to use the royal cars. Aren't they reserved for driving the royals?"

"No, we're not supposed to, but they'll never find out. If they do, I'll come up with some story. I'm a good liar. Besides, I know you like to break the rules."

Mena was offended by being called a rule-breaker but tried not to let it show. "I have only broken one."

"Well, this makes two," he said as he held the passenger door open for her.

Mena got in and fastened her seat belt. Her family was poor, so she had been in few cars in her lifetime. This car was the plushest she had been in by far. She had known the royal cars were fancy, but she didn't know cars could be this fancy.

"It's nice, isn't it?" Adam said as he got into the driver's seat.

"Yes," Mena said truthfully.

Adam started to drive. He drove off of the royal grounds and kept going through Superion City's winding streets. The city was quiet. Most of the shops and businesses had closed hours ago. Mena rarely had reason to venture away from the castle and didn't know her way around the city. If she somehow got separated from Adam, she wouldn't know how to get back.

"Where are we going?" she asked.

He glanced at her before returning his eyes to the road. "It's a surprise."

"Lovely," she said, although a surprise date with a man she didn't like was not lovely at all. The drive was quiet. Mena was unsure what to talk about, and Adam didn't make any attempts at conversation.

"We're here," Adam finally announced as he parked the car outside a red brick building. As far as Mena could tell, it looked like an ordinary house.

"Don't worry. It's a lot nicer on the inside," he said with a smile.

They got out of the car, and he led her inside. To Mena's surprise, it was a classy restaurant. Despite herself, she was impressed and wished she had been able to dress up. They were led to a table, and their waiter, an older gentleman who gave Mena a polite smile, handed them menus. The idea of someone waiting on her for a change was strange.

"Order whatever you want. It's my treat," Adam said.

Mena ordered a pasta dish that was the cheapest on the menu. She didn't want to be greedy, and the pasta was delicious. She was offered wine, but she refused. Wine was something she had never developed a taste for, and the fact that some people did odd things when they drank alcohol frightened her. Adam ordered a meal and a drink that sounded very complicated. Mena was glad she wasn't the one expected to prepare it.

She tried to be sociable. "Did you grow up in Superion City?" she asked.

"Yes, but we don't have to talk about that. And we don't have to talk about wherever you're from. I'm sure it's boring."

Mena didn't think Aurora Village, her home, was boring, but she was kind of glad not to talk about it. Even though she was fond of Frankie, she missed her family and the country. Talking about them would only make her miss them more.

Adam decided to talk cars, and he rambled on and on. Mena had no idea what he was talking about.

"Oh, I don't think the young lady wants to hear all that," the waiter said when he cleared their plates.

"Mind your own business and bring us dessert," Adam snapped.

"You didn't have to yell at him," Mena said when the waiter had left, presumably to get their dessert. She was embarrassed for the poor man.

"What? It's his job to wait on us. He knows that. I'm sure that brat of a princess gives you orders all day just like that."

"No, she doesn't, and she's not a brat."

Adam looked like he didn't believe her, but he didn't say anything more. They ate their dessert in silence. Mena hadn't thought she wanted dessert. She had already had plenty to eat, but when she saw the chocolate cake, she couldn't help herself. She loved chocolate as much as Frankie did.

"I had a very nice time. Thank you for taking me," Mena said when they got back to the car. It wasn't a complete lie. Adam wasn't the best company, but he had just treated her to what was certainly the best dinner she ever had. She just hoped she had been a satisfactory date; she hoped she had played her part well enough that he wouldn't reveal her secret.

"You're welcome," Adam said.

She expected him to start driving, but he didn't. Instead, he stared at her as if he were considering her. She forced a yawn and hoped it looked authentic.

"Goodness, it's almost morning," Mena said. "I will have to be waking Princess Frances for her lesson in a few hours. If I'm lucky, I'll get a little sleep myself when we get back to the castle."

"We don't have to hurry back to the castle. You can wait a little longer," Adam said. He leaned over and kissed her.

What was happening? Mena knew the city folks tended to move fast, but she wasn't a city girl. She was still a modest country girl at heart, and nice, modest girls didn't kiss a boy on the first date. She tried to push him away gently. He didn't seem to get the hint. She shoved him harder.

"No, it's late. We really should be getting back," she said, slightly breathless. He would probably think she was terribly uptight and old fashioned, but she couldn't worry about that. She needed to do what felt right.

"You don't mean that," he said, leaning toward her again.

"Really, I do," she said. She pulled back and tried to look as fierce as she could. She was so nervous that she felt warm all over, but she tried to give him an icy stare.

Adam glared back. Mena thought he would lunge for her again. Maybe she should get out of the car and make a run for it.

"Fine," Adam said. "I'll take you back to the castle, and you can look after that brat."

Mena said a silent prayer of gratitude when he started to drive.

CHAPTER SIX

Mena (and Zac) woke her a little earlier this morning. Frankie was grateful. She had plenty of time to dress and even eat breakfast before her lessons. She shared her toast with Zac.

As usual, Mena kept busy, but she didn't look well today. She had dark circles under her eyes, and she seemed quiet.

"Are you ill, Mena?" Frankie said.

"Oh no, I'm okay," Mena said with a weak smile. "I just had a hard time getting to sleep last night. Don't you worry about me."

Now that he had helped Frankie with her breakfast, Zac decided to eat his own breakfast. Frankie watched him. He was so cute, and he was getting even bigger.

"You had better get downstairs, Frankie," Mena said. "You don't want to be late for your lesson."

"I know, lateness is not proper for a princess," Frankie said. She might as well say it for Mena once in a while.

Frankie walked into the formal dining room and was greeted by her parents and Thomas. The tutor gave her a cheerful smile, but her parents looked stern.

"Again, we had hoped to observe your lesson, but we have been called away. We may be gone for a few days this time," Queen Veronica said.

Frankie noticed the suitcases at their feet.

"Maybe you will be Traveling by the time we get back," King Leopold said. He was hopeful, maybe a little delusional.

Like the previous day, the king and queen used their Gift of Travel to leave the castle.

Thomas turned to Frankie. "So, I thought we would work on the other Gifts today and see if those stick. What do you think?"

"Okay," Frankie said. She doubted either of the other Gifts would stick, but she didn't see any harm in trying.

"Excellent," Thomas said. He sat down at the table. "Have a seat. We will work on the Gift of the Mind first. Try to clear your mind of any chatter and let yourself be calm."

Frankie sat across from Thomas and did as she was told. She sat as still as she could without fidgeting. Even though the thoughts that these Gift lessons were silly were in her mind, she forced them down.

"I'm thinking of a color," Thomas said. "Focus on me. Try to read my thought and tell me what it is. It takes some time at first, so don't feel like you have to rush."

Frankie focused. Since Thomas had mentioned colors, she could think of a long list of colors, but she had no idea what color he was thinking of. She couldn't read his mind. Finally, Frankie decided that rather than sitting in silence, she should probably guess.

"Red?"

"No."

"Yellow?"

"No."

"Purple?"

"No."

It took several more guesses before Frankie could identify his color as green. They repeated the exercise again and again. Then Thomas said they had tried enough for today. Frankie didn't blame him for wanting to stop. She was only guessing, and all of her guesses were bad. She didn't even have one lucky guess to give some false hope.

"Do not be discouraged – " Thomas said.

"Were you thinking about grass?" Frankie blurted.

"No," Thomas said, a bit startled by Frankie's odd question.

"Sorry, I don't know where that came from," Frankie said. "One of your colors was green so that probably got me thinking about grass. I'm sorry to interrupt. What were you saying?"

"Don't be discouraged," Thomas said. "The Gift of the Mind, like all Gifts, can be difficult to harness. Just because you were struggling today doesn't mean you don't have the Gift of the Mind. Let's work on the Gift of Reach for a while. I think you're used to focusing by now."

Frankie nodded.

"Good. Put your hands on the table please."

Frankie did as she was instructed. Thomas set a pencil on the table.

"Reachers can move objects from one place to another. However, almost all Reachers learn by summoning objects to themselves," Thomas said. "Try Reaching for this pencil. Bring it to your hand."

Frankie made herself calm and focused. That part she could do. She was getting good at it actually. When the Minder training seemed unsuccessful, she could at least do something and guess. That wouldn't work with the Reacher training. She could only sit still and hope the pencil magically made its way to her fingers. Maybe a draft could come along and blow the pencil closer to her. That would at least be an illusion of progress. She glanced at the windows. They were all firmly shut. She wasn't going to get any help there, and she knew the air conditioning vents wouldn't blow on the table.

"You're cheating. You're moving your fingers," Thomas said patiently.

Frankie looked down. Her fingers had indeed started to inch forward. She pulled them back. She focused on keeping her hands still and thinking about the pencil. She felt foolish. If she was a Reacher, which she didn't believe she was, it wasn't working today. She tried not to audibly sigh with relief when Mena brought their lunch.

"Thank you, Mena. That looks wonderful," Frankie said. Today's lunch was salad with, of course, some chocolate as a treat.

"You're welcome, Princess," Mena said. "How is your lesson going?"

"Not well," Frankie said. "If I have a Gift, we haven't found it yet."

"Well, I'm sure you will. Enjoy your lunch," Mena said. She left the room. To continue on with the million chores she did each day, Frankie guessed.

"She seems nice," Thomas observed.

"Mena's the best," Frankie said. "She's my closest friend."

"You don't seem to treat her like a servant," Thomas said.

"Oh, Mena waits on me a great deal," Frankie said. "I'm hopeless at things like hair and makeup. I'm hopeless at a lot of things really. Mena helps me so much. I don't know what I would do without her."

"I know she helps you, but you don't have the superior attitude toward her that most royals have toward servants," Thomas said. "It's refreshing to see."

Frankie didn't know what to say to that. People weren't supposed to openly criticize royals, but he was doing just that right in front of her, a royal. However, he was also complimenting her on being different from most royals. Frankie quietly ate her salad. She hoped that Thomas would read his book again so that she wouldn't have to make conversation, but he did not. Even though she felt like Thomas was on her side, she didn't know what to talk about. She didn't know how to socialize with a teacher. Fortunately, he didn't seem bothered by the quiet. They ate in companionable silence. When they were finished, Thomas took out a thick history book.

"History lessons were part of your primary education, correct?" Thomas said.

"Yes," Frankie said. History had never been her favorite subject, but she didn't want to tell Thomas that part.

"What did you learn?" he said.

"We always learned about Superion, mostly about the royals. They always started with the present royal family and worked backwards. It's strange learning about yourself in class. The lessons never seemed very objective. They always talked about how great royals were, which can't be accurate. Nobody can be as perfect as they made the royals out to be. We never covered much though. Each year we learned about the most recent generations of royals. Then school was finished for the year. It got boring after a while."

"I thought that would be the case," Thomas said. "That is the standard practice in almost all primary schools in Superion. I believe a lot can be learned from the past, so that's what we're going to do here. We're going to be starting as far back as we can and work our way forward."

Frankie liked that idea. She liked to learn, and she would be having her first fresh history lesson in years. "So we're starting with the early days of Superion?"

"Unfortunately, we cannot start with the very first days of Superion. It is thought that the kingdom of Superion used to be part of Allton. Maybe there was some kind of conflict. In any case, they didn't have many records then, so we can't discuss that. We will be going back as far as we can, to the first royal family that there is record of."

Their history lesson lasted all afternoon with Frankie listening intently. She learned that there were many differences between the Superion she knew and the Superion of long ago. A major difference was how the royal family became the royal family.

"Why is your family the royal family, Frankie?" Thomas asked.

"Because it keeps getting passed down," she said. "That's what we learn in school."

"Exactly. It keeps getting passed down from generation to generation. If there wasn't a direct descendent, a distant relation was found. Great care has been taken to keep your family in power. Please understand that I'm not criticizing your family, but royalty was a much different concept years ago. The royal family was elected, and they would each serve Superion for their given amount of time."

"You mean they would just stop being royalty after a few years?" Frankie said. This concept was strange to her. Even though she had never asked to be a royal, she was a royal for life, unless her parents decided to send her away.

"Yes, some went back to being ordinary citizens after a few years. Others stayed in power longer, but it wasn't only their choice to stay in power. They were voted on by the citizens."

"Did they miss being royalty?"

"Yes, I suppose some did, but they always went back to being ordinary citizens when their time was up. Those were the rules."

Frankie learned that the attitudes between Gifted and Not Gifted were also much different. While she didn't agree with it, she was used to the Gifted looking down on the Not Gifted, with the Not Gifted being bitter in return.

"I cannot be certain, but it looks like there weren't always Gifts in Superion," Thomas said. "No one knows what caused some people to be Gifted, but all of a sudden people started to have these extra abilities. People were frightened at first. They thought the Gifts were unnatural and a sickness. Then they started to learn that whatever had caused the Gifts, the Gifts could benefit society and were considered a blessing.

The Gifted were cherished for the special things they could do, but there wasn't the great divide between the Gifted and Not Gifted like there is today. Even though the Gifted and Not Gifted had different abilities, they each contributed to society and were considered equal. They had similar lifestyles and earned similar wages."

Frankie found this interesting. She had often wondered about the rules and attitudes in Superion and was intrigued to find out that the world as she knew it hadn't always been that way.

"That sounds nice. It sounds more fair than what we have today," Frankie said. "But how did things change so much? What happened?"

Thomas looked disappointed. "I wish I could tell you. I would expect that things changed gradually over time. That seems logical as most change is gradual. Although, I wonder if there was an event to so drastically change Superion's thinking. Superion's history has holes in it. As I said, there are no mentions of Superion's earliest history. It sounds like there have been other sporadic events that have been deleted from the records, things someone didn't want found out."

Frankie couldn't help herself. "Why?"

"Many scholars have tried to figure that out but have been unsuccessful. Whoever wanted pieces of Superion's history to be hidden really made sure to hide it."

Frankie's favorite part of the lesson involved animals. The primary school lessons had rarely included animals.

"People rely on animals quite a bit. First, animals can be food," Thomas said.

Without meaning to, Frankie made a face.

"I have eaten with you for a few days now, and I noticed that you don't eat meat, do you?" Thomas said.

Frankie shook her head.

"Why is that?"

"Because I like animals. I wouldn't feel right knowing animals died so that I could eat." She had explained this to her parents many times, but they thought she was foolish.

"That reasoning makes a lot of sense. There are others that share that belief today. Not a lot, but some. That was a popular opinion in the past. People were much more connected to animals then. They relied on animals for milk and eggs. Some people ate meat, but it was rare. Animals were also relied on for clothing. Sometimes the animal had to be killed to make it into clothing but not always. Cows need to be killed to be made into leather, but sheep are merely shorn for their wool. People also valued animals for their companionship as pets in the past. Some people keep pets today, but it was a much more common practice in the past."

Frankie knew firsthand what a good companion a dog could be. She was tempted to tell Thomas so, but she couldn't tell him about Zac. She couldn't tell too many people her secret.

"Perhaps the biggest contribution that animals made to society," Thomas said, "was they could be trained to serve."

Frankie was fascinated as Thomas taught her about service animals. Zac was cute and a good buddy, but Frankie had never imagined that dogs like him were once police officers, guides, and helpers for the sick. It had to be her favorite lesson ever, and she was disappointed when Thomas announced they were finished for the day.

"Don't look so glum," Thomas said. "Our lessons can't last all day. I need to get home to my family, and I'm sure you would like to eat dinner and play. I'll be back tomorrow."

"Can we have another animal lesson tomorrow?" Frankie asked hopefully.

"I hadn't expected you to be so interested in animals. Yes, I can prepare some more animal lessons for you, but we can't forget your other subjects. Your parents hired me to instruct you in a well-rounded education."

Thomas put his heavy books back in his bag and stood.

"Good night, Princess. I will be going," he said.

"Good night. Thank you for my lesson."

Frankie expected Thomas to leave the room. Instead, he stood still with his bag over his shoulder and his eyes closed. She was about to ask him if anything was wrong, but then she remembered that he specialized in Traveler training, which most likely meant that he was a Traveler himself. She was so used to seeing her parents Travel that she often forgot most Travelers were not able to Travel as quickly as they were. It took Thomas a few minutes of focus, but then he disappeared.

** ** **

Zac was getting used to the routines of the castle. He spent the days with Mena who he liked very much, and then he spent the evenings with Frankie who he loved. At night, he got to sleep in the super soft bed with Frankie. Mena was very nice and took good care of him, and Frankie was his hero.

Zac was excited to see Frankie return to their room this evening.

She bent down to pet him, and he gave her kisses.

"I learned about dogs today, Zac," Frankie said. "It was a great lesson. You probably would have liked it."

Zac was curious. He had never been to a lesson and wasn't sure what that was, but he would love to go to a lesson with Frankie. He would love to go anywhere with Frankie.

"I'm glad you're enjoying some of your lessons, Frankie," Mena said. "Dinner is ready."

Dinner was indeed ready. Frankie ate sitting at the table, and Zac ate out of a bowl on the floor. Frankie's dinner was all vegetables. Zac liked some vegetables. Carrots were his favorite. His dinner tonight was carrots and hamburger. Mena didn't eat anything at all; Zac wondered why that was.

Frankie set down her fork. She was finished eating. "I need to go for a walk," she said. "I've been sitting all day, and my legs want to move. I'll take Zac with me."

Zac's ears perked up, and his tail started to wag. He was going somewhere with Frankie!

"Do be careful!" Mena said.

"I'm always careful, but you can come with us if you like," Frankie said. "You can keep me out of trouble."

"I don't know if I can do that, but I think I will go with you. I could use some fresh air myself," Mena said.

Zac was put into the bag, which he was used to even if he didn't particularly like it. At least they were going somewhere! When they got a little bit away from the castle, Zac was taken from the bag and set on the ground. He had the leash on and was allowed to walk next to Frankie. Zac noticed that Frankie had a green scarf covering her head. He thought she looked prettier without it, but maybe she was cold. Zac didn't know where they were, but Frankie led the way.

"Who wants ice cream?" Frankie said. Zac didn't know what ice cream was, but if it was food, he would have some. He loved to eat.

"I'd better not, but you go ahead," Mena said.

"Don't be silly," Frankie said. "You must be starving. You never eat dinner until about midnight since you won't eat until after I go to bed. What's your favorite flavor?"

"Chocolate," Mena said reluctantly.

Frankie bought three dishes of ice cream from a shop. She and Mena had chocolate. She bought a small dish of something called vanilla ice cream for Zac because chocolate was bad for dogs. Vanilla ice cream was the best thing Zac had ever eaten! He wished Frankie had bought him a bigger dish.

After they ate their ice cream, they walked a little bit further through the winding streets. Zac began to recognize the neighborhood they were in. There were a lot of animals here. They were near the mean old man's house. Zac wasn't as afraid of the mean old man with Frankie here. Frankie would protect him. They passed a house where they kept cats, then a house where they kept horses. When they got to a house where they kept sheep, there was a terrible sight. They all stopped in horror. Zac let out a whimper.

CHAPTER SEVEN

Mena was glad she had agreed to come for the walk. She rarely got a chance to see Superion City. Even though she was allowed some free time to herself now and then, she usually spent that time in her room. She was too nervous to venture around the city on her own. Frankie was a good guide. She knew her way around so well. Mena wasn't surprised. Frankie spent so much time adventuring. Frankie led them to the southern edge of the city. Mena enjoyed seeing the different animals here and there; it reminded her of home. They all stopped when they saw the sheep. Instead of grazing peacefully, the sheep were all dead.

"Who did this to them?" Frankie asked in a whisper.

"Animals die," Mena said gently. "You know they use sheep for wool."

"But they don't need to kill them for the wool," Frankie said.

Mena knew this, but she didn't think Frankie would. "They may have killed them for food. Some people eat lamb," Mena said.

"No, that doesn't make sense," Frankie said. "This doesn't look like it was done for any practical purpose. It was too violent. These sheep were murdered."

Mena didn't want to admit it, but Frankie was probably right. The scene really was heartbreaking. Sheep were such peaceful animals, and there was so much blood. The sight made Mena nauseous. She had to look away.

"We should get back to the castle, Frankie."

"Not yet. I want to know who did this," Frankie said. A small crowd of people had gathered, and Frankie started toward them.

"No, don't!" Mena said in a low voice. "You wait over here. I'll go."

Thankfully, Frankie listened. Mena went to join the group. Frankie was braver than she was, but Frankie was recognizable. Even with her head covered, people might still recognize the princess, and the princess shouldn't be caught out here asking questions. Mena was no one, and in her black servant dress, she blended in.

"Brought it on himself. Causing too much trouble," a man was saying.

"What happened?" Mena asked an older woman.

"The king and queen," she said.

Mena gasped. "The king and queen did this?"

"Don't look so surprised," the woman said. "They have been doing things like this all over the kingdom. They do it to punish the people who speak out." She gave a barky cough. She was pale and looked very tired. "This fellow had been making a big fuss over wanting more money for his work. I don't blame him for wanting more, but he should have kept his mouth shut. Now all of his sheep are dead, and he's in prison. Don't get me wrong. I think we Not Gifted deserve better than we get, but I would rather be a poor second-class citizen than in prison."

Mena carried two mugs of hot cocoa into the princess's room. She had eaten ice cream with the princess earlier, and now she was joining her for hot cocoa. It wasn't at all proper behavior for a maid. She knew Frankie didn't care. Frankie would never correct her behavior. Maybe Mena shouldn't be so hard on herself either. They had witnessed an awful scene, and despite the summer heat outside, Mena felt chilled to the bone. The situation definitely justified hot cocoa with the princess.

Mena set the mugs on the table and sat down across from Frankie. The walk home to the castle had been a brisk and quiet one. They had barely said a word. Mena didn't know what to say now either. She had a lot of respect for the king and queen, but this evening's experience had left her shaken. She sipped her hot cocoa.

"I can't believe they did that to that man," Frankie said, breaking the silence. "The prison part isn't so bad. I mean, he shouldn't have gone to prison just for speaking his mind, but at least he will get out at some point. They can't hold him forever. But those poor sheep. They're all dead. They didn't do anything to deserve that. They're innocent sheep!"

Mena couldn't agree more. As far as she was concerned, there was no reason for such cruelty. She wished she could say something to comfort Frankie.

"You know the king and queen hate animals," Mena said. "This was just the first time we actually witnessed it." She knew it wasn't a good explanation.

Zac cuddled up in Frankie's lap, and Frankie rubbed his soft fur. "I don't think I want to be a royal anymore," she sighed. "Not if it means associating with them."

There was a knock at the door. The girls exchanged a worried look. No one ever looked for Princess Frances. Except for being expected to attend her lessons and royal functions, she was all but forgotten in the castle.

Mena set down her mug. She stood and smoothed her skirt. "Who is it?" she called.

"I'm looking for Mena," a gruff voice said.

Mena froze. She knew that voice. Why was he looking for her? She had kept her promise. Now why couldn't he leave her to do her job and wait on the princess in peace? She was about to tell Frankie to hide Zac, but Frankie was way ahead of her. Zac was already tucked away in the wardrobe.

Adam burst into the room.

"Excuse me!" Mena said. "What do you think you're doing, barging into the princess's room? That is highly inappropriate!" Mena tried to sound stern and angry, but she was frightened. Her voice shook slightly.

"Oh, like you care what's appropriate," Adam sneered.

"I care that you're in my room, and I want you out!" Frankie said hotly.

Adam looked at Frankie like she was being an annoying child. He didn't look at all contrite for invading the princess's privacy. "I don't care about you," he said to Frankie. "I came here with a message for your soon to be ex-maid.

"As soon as the king and queen come back, I'm telling them your secret," Adam said meanly, proud of himself.

"But I did what you wanted. I went on a date with you," Mena pleaded. She fought back tears.

"Ew, you went on a date with this creep?" Frankie said.

Adam shook his head. "Not good enough," he said. "You think all I'm interested in is a girl to eat dinner with? Not at all good enough."

Frankie stomped her foot. "Leave her alone! Get out!"

"I take it you heard about those sheep today," Adam said to Frankie. "When your parents come back, that's what they'll do to that mutt, and I'll laugh as you cry about it."

Mena watched as in an instant, Frankie's annoyance at Adam turned into rage. Slight as she was, she used all of her strength to punch Adam square in the jaw. Dazed, he staggered backward into the hall.

"Leave us alone!" Frankie yelled. Then she slammed and locked the door.

"It's all my fault. I never meant for anyone to find out about Zac," Mena said. She was once again sitting with Frankie and Zac. She had just told Frankie the story of Adam seeing her with Zac and the deal of the date.

"No, it's not your fault," Frankie said. "Someone was bound to find out eventually. I was a fool to think I could keep a dog here."

Even though Frankie wasn't angry with her, Mena still felt terrible. She drank the last of her now cold cocoa. "I should go. The king and queen will fire me anyway," she said. "I'll take Zac with me. I'll keep him safe."

Zac pawed at Frankie's chair. She lifted him up onto her lap. "Why do you and Zac get to go? I want to go."

"Don't be silly. I would love your company, but I don't even know where I'm going. I can try to find work in the city, but I may have to go back up north with my family. That is no life for a princess."

"I don't care about being a princess. I can run away. Kids run away all the time."

"You may not care about being a princess, but you are a princess. Lots of kids run away, but the princess can't. There would be a search all over the kingdom. All of Superion would know about it. There would probably be a reward for your return too, so people would really want to find you. A runaway princess is just not realistic."

"Maybe not," Frankie said glumly.

Mena was about to tidy up and put everyone to bed when she saw movement across the room. She stopped. It couldn't be.

"Frankie, did you start a fire?"

"What? No."

They both stared at the stone fireplace where a small fire burned. Even though it was cold, they couldn't have a fire. If King Leopold found out, he would be furious. There were to be no efforts to warm the castle in the summertime; it was one of the first things Mena had been told upon being hired. Mena quickly extinguished the fire. She wondered how it had started. Oh well. She couldn't worry about it. She had enough to worry about as it was.

"Time for bed, Frankie. You have a lesson tomorrow."

"Okay," Frankie said. "I may not be able to run away, but I have another idea."

CHAPTER EIGHT

"Good morning," Frankie said brightly. She stood in the dining room. The king and queen were still away, so she greeted Thomas by herself this morning.

"Good morning, Frankie," Thomas said. "How are you today?"

"Okay, I guess. Mena and I are in a bit of trouble though. Could you help us?"

Thomas sat down at the table and looked at Frankie thoughtfully. "What kind of trouble?"

Frankie took her seat across from him. She told him the whole story, starting with how she had gotten Zac.

"Now I understand why you were so interested in the animal lesson yesterday," Thomas said. "Mena is right. You can't run away. How do you expect me to help?"

"I should bring Mena in. This affects her as much as it does me." Frankie stood and walked over to a series of buttons on the wall. The buttons sent signals to the castle's staff. Frankie rarely used the signals, but she pushed the button to signal Mena now.

Mena entered the room a few minutes later. "You rang for me, Princess?"

"I'm trying to get Thomas to help us. Let's tell him our idea," Frankie said.

"Your idea," Mena corrected. She hesitantly joined Frankie and Thomas at the table and gave Thomas a shy hello.

"I think you should take me away to study," Frankie said. "Kids go away to study. If you tell my parents it's for the best, they'll believe you. Maybe tell them you think I'll focus better outside of the castle."

"Where do you propose I take you?" Thomas said.

"Anywhere. Where do you and your family live?" Frankie said. It was rude to just invite herself in. "I'm sure my parents would pay my expenses. I really don't want to intrude," she added quickly.

"We live in the north," Thomas said. "I would be happy to have you, but we have a small house. I don't know where we would put the three of you."

"Excuse me. What do you mean three?" Mena said. "Frankie needs someplace to stay while she does her lessons, and she will want to keep Zac with her. He's her dog. He should stay with her. But you don't need to worry about me. I can find a way for myself. I'll find employment and a place to live."

"Nonsense, Mena. I will worry about you," Thomas said. "You are Frankie's friend. You should stay together. I can't make any promises, but I will try to help you find employment in the north."

"Where in the north?" Mena said.

Then Mena and Thomas had a discussion about northern geography that Frankie had a hard time following. She had been to the north before. Her parents had taken her there on royal business, but the downside of having Traveler parents who could whisk her away anywhere was that she lost a sense of geography. It turned out that Thomas and Mena were from the same village, Aurora. They were practically neighbors.

"Would you like to stay with my family, Frankie?" Mena offered. "Our home isn't anywhere near as fancy as the castle, but we could make room for you and Zac."

"That sounds perfect," Frankie said, delighted.

"I think we have a plan," Thomas said. "I can't believe I'm helping a princess to escape, but there you have it. When do we leave?"

"Tomorrow," Frankie said. Now that the plan was set, why delay it?

"Why wait that long?" Thomas said. "Do you know when the king and queen will return?"

"No, they didn't say," Frankie said.

"Then we better leave today," Thomas said.

"How are we going to get there?" Mena said, always thinking of practical things. "Do you have a car? The royal driver won't take us, and it's probably better that he doesn't know where we are anyway."

"No, from what you've told me about him, he doesn't sound like a trustworthy fellow," Thomas said.

"We don't need a driver," Frankie said. "Thomas is a Traveler."

Thomas looked at Frankie sadly. "You are forgetting that not all

64

Travelers are as powerful as your parents. I cannot take others with me when I Travel. However, I do have a son with a car. I can get a message to him and let him know that it is urgent. I expect he will be here in the afternoon. In the meantime, you girls better go pack."

"What about my lesson?" Frankie said.

"We will have plenty of time for lessons in Aurora," Thomas said. "Today we are traveling, just not the Gifted way."

** ** **

Zac jerked his head up with a start. He had been napping, but now someone was here. Mena was here! Frankie was here too! Frankie was never back this early. This was really a treat! Zac ran over to Frankie, and she petted him.

"You're going on an adventure, Zac," she said.

Zac wagged his tail. He liked the sound of that.

The girls were very busy. They piled things into a case.

"I've never stayed anywhere overnight before," Frankie said.

"Really?" Mena said. "I thought the royals traveled all over the kingdom."

"Yes, but when your parents are Travelers, there's no need to stay overnight. My parents always brought me home so that I could sleep in my own bed. I have no idea what I'm supposed to pack."

"Clothes," Mena said.

Zac noticed that it was mostly Mena putting Frankie's things in the case. Frankie just added soft things here and there like pajamas and socks.

"Well yes, but do I really need all those dresses?" Frankie said. "There shouldn't be any royal functions in Aurora that I'm expected to go to. I'm just taking lessons."

"You will need plenty of dresses even if we're not bringing your nicest ones," Mena said. "What else would you wear to your lessons?"

"Pajamas," Frankie suggested.

"You can wear pajamas for sleeping, not for your lessons," Mena said. "You don't wear pajamas for your lessons here, do you? My goodness, sometimes I feel like I'm looking after a little sister and not the princess."

Frankie seemed to give up on packing. She sat on the bed next to Zac. It looked like Mena was the expert on packing anyway.

"I think that's it," Mena announced a few minutes later. "My bag is downstairs; I packed it last night."

"What about Zac? Does he need a bag?" Frankie asked.

"No," Mena said. "He will wear his collar and leash. There's no need to bring food for him. We will get food there. He really doesn't have anything to bring."

Zac didn't agree with this. He did have something to bring. He got his teddy bear and put it in the suitcase.

** ** **

Frankie sat in the castle's entrance hall as patiently as she could. This was it. She couldn't believe it. She was leaving the castle. She had thought she would live here forever. Sitting still was a challenge. She wanted to pace. The movement would make her feel better, but it would probably make Mena nervous.

Mena had stationed herself at the window to look for the first sign of the car. "I think this is them," she said.

Frankie gripped Zac's leash tightly and joined Mena at the window. Her breath caught when a guard stopped the car. She prayed the guard wouldn't give Thomas and his son any trouble. The guards knew Thomas was her tutor. Her parents had given him permission to be in the castle. She finally exhaled when the car was allowed to proceed to the castle's door.

Mena opened the door for Thomas and his son. Strangely, the younger Mr. Tate looked familiar to Frankie. He had dark hair and was a bit older than Mena. Why would she know him though? She couldn't have met him before. Then she remembered.

"You were my Test Administrator," Frankie said.

"Yes, I was. It's nice to see you again, Princess Frances," he said.

"Thank you for driving us, sir. This is very kind of you," Mena said.

"You are welcome," he said. "But please don't call me sir. You can call me David, and you must be Mena."

Mena nodded shyly.

Zac gave a hello bark.

"This is Zac," Frankie said for him.

David bent down to pet Zac. "This is the dog these nice girls are escaping the castle for. You are a very special dog. Well, we had better get going. I would like to make it there before dark if we can."

David and his father helped the girls carry their bags. They were almost out the door when they had company. By the Gift of Travel, the king and queen arrived in the entrance hall.

"I think that was a productive trip. I – " Queen Veronica froze when she saw Frankie and her friends.

"What's all this? Where are you going?" King Leopold demanded.

Before Frankie could respond, Thomas jumped to the rescue. He quickly explained that he must take Frankie to Aurora for her studies at once, that most students learned their Gifts away from the distractions of home, that surely the castle must hold many distractions for Frankie.

King Leopold seemed to consider this argument. Frankie wished they had gotten out the door just a few minutes earlier. If only they had left before the king and queen had gotten here, they could have avoided this!

"Fine," King Leopold said after a long moment. "But you must keep me up to date on Frankie's progress. I want frequent updates. Is Mena going as well? That is good. Frankie will need someone to look after her."

This was working out much better than Frankie would have anticipated. She would have expected a scene.

"What is that? What is it doing in my castle?" Queen Veronica shrieked hysterically. She pointed at Zac and tried to get far away from him as quickly as she could.

There was the scene Frankie expected. She looked down at Zac as if she wanted him to come up with a fib and fast.

"He's mine," David fibbed smoothly. "I'm sorry, Queen Veronica. I didn't know you didn't like dogs. He's a great companion for me, and he loves the car. I thought Princess Frances and Mena would like him. My apologies again."

Frankie sat in the back seat with Mena and Zac. This was the first car she had ever been in that was not a royal car. The difference was obvious. This car was nowhere near as plush. Frankie didn't care about plush though. As long as this car was able to get her to her destination, she was happy. As much as she loved to walk and run, they were traveling a long way.

Something had been on Frankie's mind for the last little bit. "David, why were you my Test Administrator?"

"I was asked to be a Test Administrator by the school," David said. "The schools organize the Test each year, overseen by the king and queen of course. They asked me because I'm a doctor. With the Test being a blood analysis, they like to have doctors administer it. The fact that I was your Test Administrator and now we meet again is quite the coincidence, isn't it?"

"Indeed," Frankie agreed. "Speaking of the Test, do you think mine was correct? It said I was Gifted, but I don't believe it. I have been practicing all of the Gifts, and I don't have a single one. I think I'm Not Gifted, not like that would be so bad."

"Your result was abnormal, but the Test doesn't lie," David said. "I think you are Gifted. You just haven't discovered it yet."

CHAPTER NINE

Mena gazed out the window at the passing farms. Aurora Village was at the northernmost tip of the Kingdom of Superion. It was as far away from Superion City as you could get without leaving the kingdom. The drive to Aurora was a long but pretty one. Mena hadn't expected to be going home so soon. Getting a job in Superion Castle had been a dream come true. If you were Not Gifted, working as a servant in the castle was one of the best jobs in the kingdom. Mena had hoped to work there many years. She hadn't expected events to take the turn that they had.

Mena's emotions were all over the place. She was excited to go home to her parents and her house. An honor as it was to live and work in the castle, it wasn't home. She was also worried. Yes, the king and queen were happy to have her look after Frankie, but they hadn't heard Adam's story yet. As soon as Adam told them (and he would definitely do so as soon as possible), Mena would surely be fired. Finding work was hard. She hoped Thomas would keep his promise and help her if he could; he seemed like a nice man. Then what would happen to Frankie when Mena was fired? Frankie was smart and brave, but she needed someone to look after her.

"Are you paying attention, Mena?"

"I'm sorry. What was that?" Mena had been so deep in her thoughts that she had apparently missed Frankie talking to her.

"We're playing a game. I'm guessing the animals, and Thomas is telling me about them."

Thomas chuckled. "I've never done a mobile lesson. I've never met a student who was so reluctant to have a day off," he said ruefully.

"Do you want to play?" Frankie asked Mena.

"Okay," Mena said.

They took turns identifying the animals, and Mena had to admit that she was enjoying Thomas' commentary. It was a game and a lesson rolled into one. It was good for Frankie because it kept her up with her studies; it was good for Mena because it kept her mind off her worries some. Frankie seemed intrigued by the farms and animals. Mena didn't blame her. Frankie was so used to the castle and the city; this was like a different world.

"I hate to interrupt, but we're almost there," David said. David was handsome. Mena scolded herself for thinking it. He was a doctor; he was far above a servant girl like herself. "Is this your street, Mena?"

"Yes, third house on the right," Mena said. She hoped no one noticed her blushing.

Mena assured Thomas and David they didn't need to wait. It really wasn't necessary, but this would probably be better without a crowd. With Frankie and Zac, it was a small crowd already. Mena still had her key; she let them in.

"Who's there?" Anna called.

"It's just me, Mom," Mena replied.

Her parents rushed to meet her at the door. "Mena? What are you doing here? Did something happen at the castle?" Anna said. Her parents were surprised to have her home, but they were even more surprised that she wasn't alone. They stared at the princess in wonder. "You have brought the princess here," Anna said. "It's an honor to meet you, Princess Frances."

The front hallway of Mena's house was nothing like the entrance hall of Superion Castle. You could host a party in the castle's entrance hall, but this hallway felt crowded with the few of them standing there. It made Mena nervous. She hoped this would work out.

"You can call me Frankie," the princess said, as she usually did.

Zac gave a bark.

"And this is my friend Zac," Frankie added.

"Can we get you anything? Would you like some dinner?" Anna asked.

"Yes, dinner would be wonderful. I'm starving," Frankie said. "Actually, if it's not too much trouble, Zac and I need somewhere to stay. We would love to stay here with Mena if that's okay. Is it okay? Would it be terribly inconvenient?" Mena would have worked up to that, but not Frankie. Frankie was much bolder.

"Oh my, the princess stay with us?" Anna said, flustered.

"We would be happy to have you, Frankie," Don jumped in. "Make yourself at home."

The girls put their bags in Mena's room. Then Mena helped her mother prepare dinner. Frankie offered to help, but Anna insisted she relax. Frankie sat down at the kitchen table with Zac in her lap.

Don sat down across from her. "So Frankie, what brings you to Aurora Village?"

"My lessons," Frankie said. "I just started secondary school, and my parents have me working with a tutor. His name is Thomas Tate. He is very nice. He thought my studies would go better away from the castle."

"Thomas Tate. I don't think I know him. He must not have a sweet tooth," Don said.

"We own a bakery. The only way we know someone is if they have a sweet tooth," Anna explained.

"Frankie loves sweets," Mena said with a grin as she chopped the vegetables.

"Then she'll like it here," Don said. "What do you think of Aurora Village so far, Frankie? It must be a change from the big city, isn't it?"

"Yes, it's a lot different from the city, but I think I will like it here in Aurora Village," Frankie said.

Dinner was chicken and vegetables. Mena made sure Frankie's plate was all vegetables. Frankie set Zac on the floor when it was time to eat. Zac was not forgotten. Mena made sure he had food and water.

Throughout dinner, Don and Anna peppered Frankie with questions. They asked her about her studies, about the princess herself, about the king and queen, and about the castle. Frankie answered all of the questions patiently. So many questions would have made Mena anxious, but answering lots of questions must be normal for a royal. The topic of Mena's imminent dismissal from the castle didn't come up. Mena was grateful. She didn't want her parents to have to worry about that.

Anna insisted on giving Frankie seconds. "You're a growing girl," she said as she filled Frankie's plate with chicken and vegetables. Mena was surprised to see the chicken disappearing from Frankie's plate. Frankie never ate chicken. Then Mena realized Frankie was sneaking the chicken to Zac under the table.

After dinner, Mena sent Frankie and Zac out on a walk. She had always worried when Frankie went for walks in the city, certain that Frankie would get into mischief. She didn't have to worry about that here. Aurora Village was such a quiet place. Frankie would have to try pretty hard to find mischief here.

Mena insisted on cleaning up the kitchen for her mother.

"I can't believe the princess is staying here with us," Anna said. "I just wish you would have given us some warning. We could have tried to clean up some more and maybe gotten something special in."

"Everything looks fine," Mena said. "And there really was no time to send word. The decision was made this morning that Frankie should go away to study, and we packed our bags. That was it."

"Are you happy there? Do you like the castle?" her mother asked. People were always so curious when it came to royals and the castle. Even though her mother had asked Frankie a million questions over dinner, she wanted to hear more. People always thought of Superion Castle as a mysterious and exotic place. Mena must be getting used to it; she didn't find it all that mysterious anymore. It was just a place where people lived their lives, even if it was much fancier than the house she had grown up in.

Mena started to dry the dishes. "It's nice," she said. "It's very plush. The king and queen are fair to the staff, and Frankie really is a dear. I don't know if I can get used to the city life though. Things are so busy and loud. Maybe I'm too used to the country."

"You can get used to the city too," Anna said. "Now where will the princess sleep tonight?"

"She will sleep in my bed, of course," Mena said. "I can make a bed on the floor."

** ** **

This was awesome! Zac must be a very lucky dog to go on adventures with the princess. Most dogs didn't get to go on adventures, let alone with the princess.

The adventure had started before they had even left the castle. Zac had met the king and queen for the first time. They had used the Gift of Travel. Zac had heard of the Gift of Travel, but that was the first time he had seen anyone use that Gift. It was scary, or maybe it was the king and queen who were scary. They didn't seem nice at all. Zac was glad he had been kept a secret from them.

Then there had been the car ride. Zac had never been in a car before. The ride had been long and had made Zac feel sick. It had been a little scary too. At least Zac had Frankie and other nice humans for company on the car ride. Zac liked Thomas and David, he decided.

Zac liked Mena's parents. Mena's parents were much nicer than Frankie's parents. This was a nice house they were staying in. It wasn't big like the castle, but it was safe.

The favorite part of the day had been when Frankie had taken him for a walk. This was like a whole other world up here! Everything was so open, and there was so much grass. Zac had sniffed a lot. He wanted to sniff as much as he could to learn about this place. There were other animals nearby. Zac had seen another dog, but he had been too shy to say hello.

Now it was time for bed. As usual, Zac was cuddled up close to Frankie. This bed was nowhere near as soft and cozy as Frankie's bed in the castle, but that was okay with Zac. As long as he got to be with Frankie, he was happy. Actually, it was not a real bed at all. It was a nest of blankets on the floor. Mena was sleeping in the same room as them, and she was sleeping in a real bed. Frankie had insisted on sleeping here. Zac thought he understood why. Frankie was doing something nice for Mena. Frankie did nice things for people, and she especially did nice things for Zac.

CHAPTER TEN

Frankie felt a little disoriented when she woke up. It was strange waking up somewhere that wasn't the castle. Plus, she was the first one awake; that never happened. Mena and Zac usually had to wake her up. She blamed the sunlight pouring in through the windows. That wasn't something she was used to. She was used to thick curtains that blocked out the outside world.

Frankie tried to lie still and quiet. It was too early to be awake; she didn't want to wake Mena or Zac. She couldn't help thinking that the previous evening hadn't been all that different from her usual evenings in the castle. She had eaten dinner, which she did every evening, but she had company. Mena had actually eaten with her, which was nice. Frankie liked that Mena's parents included her in the conversation, even if they did ask a lot of questions. It was better than not being allowed to speak as was the case on the rare occasions that she ate meals with her own parents. Frankie had showered like she did at the castle, but this shower didn't have as much hot water as she was used to. Mena had adjusted it for her, but this shower wasn't as high tech. Instead of pushing buttons when she wanted shampoo and soap, Frankie had to pour them out of bottles. Mena had carefully combed and blow dried her hair as she always did. Then they had eaten some cake that Mena's mother, Anna, had baked. They didn't have Frankie's favorite treat, hot cocoa. Apparently hot cocoa wasn't popular here in the summer. That was likely because there was no air conditioning. Frankie actually welcomed the heat. It was nice not to freeze in the summertime.

Zac started to stir next to Frankie. He seemed happy today, but he always seemed happy. He also seemed hungry. Frankie didn't know why she could sense these things. It was probably because he was a growing puppy with a usually wagging tail; the description of happy and hungry had to be pretty obvious.

"Good morning, Zac," Frankie whispered.

Zac gave her kisses in response.

Frankie would let Mena sleep in. Mena deserved to sleep in once in a while. Frankie dressed as quietly as she could – in a light blue dress because Mena said it was inappropriate to wear pajamas to lessons. She pulled her hair back into a bun. It didn't look as neat as when Mena did it, but it would do.

She and Zac ventured out to the kitchen to find breakfast; Frankie was hungry too. Since Mena was sleeping, she wondered if it would be rude to serve herself, but it turned out they were not the first ones up after all. Mena's parents were already up and eating breakfast. It shouldn't be a surprise; they had to go to their jobs at the bakery.

"Good morning, Frankie," Anna said. "Can I get you some breakfast? I can make you something if you like."

"Good morning," Frankie said. She saw they were eating toast. "Toast would be great."

"Are you sure?" Anna said. "I can make you sausage or ham if you want."

"Zac would love ham, and Frankie's favorite breakfast is oatmeal," Mena said, sneaking up behind her. "I can get it."

"I was trying to let you sleep in," Frankie said. She had been so quiet too. She took a seat at the table.

"Well, it didn't work. I am trained to look after you," Mena said.

"Don't forget the meeting is today," Don said as he shuffled some papers. Anna nodded. Frankie didn't know what the meeting was, but she figured it was best not to be curious. It also seemed like whatever the papers were, Don was trying to prevent Frankie from seeing them. This made Frankie even more curious, but she ate her oatmeal quietly. The oatmeal was perfect; Mena put just the right amount of cinnamon in it as always.

"I can walk you to your lesson, Frankie," Mena offered when Frankie's oatmeal bowl was empty.

"Can Zac come?" Frankie said.

"He can walk with us, but he can't stay. He would be too much of a distraction."

Mena and Zac left her with David.

"My dad will be with you in a minute," David said. "He had someone drop by unexpectedly. If you will excuse me, I have to get to work. There are always ill people to take care of. Have a good lesson."

With that, Frankie was waiting by herself outside of Thomas' office. She sat down on the couch. Thomas hadn't been lying when he said his house was small. Mena's house was small, but there had been room for

Frankie and Zac to make a bed and sleep comfortably. Here there was barely room to stand and walk. Frankie tried to mind her own business as she waited, but whoever was in Thomas' office was shouting.

"We have to unite. The Not Gifted are getting too loud! Someone has to put them down!" a man was yelling.

If Frankie hadn't known better, she would have guessed the man was her father. Whoever he was, he certainly hated the Not Gifted as much as King Leopold did.

The man stormed out of the office a moment later. He was large and red faced. He sneered at Frankie.

"You think I'm hateful, but I'm right. The Gifted are superior. You will all see," he said before going outside.

"I'm sorry, Frankie," Thomas said. "He shouldn't have done that."

"Done what?" Frankie said.

"He read your thoughts. He's a Minder, and one of the worst sort," Thomas said.

"Oh," was all Frankie could manage. She figured her distaste was clear on her face; there would have been no reason for the Minder to read her thoughts. She was reminded that Minders probably read her thoughts every day, and she was completely oblivious to it. Geez, Minders were creepy.

"Come on," Thomas said. "Let's get started with your lesson. We will try Traveling again."

Frankie followed Thomas into his office. A table and chairs stood in the middle of the room. The walls were lined with shelves of books, and there were even stacks of books on the floor. Thomas' office was like a miniature library.

Frankie stood in a corner of the room. This room was significantly smaller than the formal dining room of the castle. If she was a Traveler at all, she should be able to Travel here. Frankie closed her eyes and focused. She had been doing well with focusing, but today it was a challenge. She eventually decided to speak up.

"I have a question. I wasn't trying to eavesdrop, but that man was very loud. What was he talking about, uniting against the Not Gifted?"

Thomas sighed. "I'm sorry you had to hear that. He is no friend of mine, but his message is clear. He is organizing a hate group. You have probably heard that some Not Gifted are pushing for higher wages."

Frankie nodded. Her parents had been talking about it, and she couldn't forget the scene with the sheep just a few days earlier.

"People like that man are strongly opposed to the Not Gifted receiving higher wages. You can see the inequalities in our society. The Not Gifted want to be equal, but there are Gifted who think they are so much better and just want to put the Not Gifted down so they can get ahead. Then, there are Gifted who use their Gifts for good and don't understand why the divide has to be so great. It seems like these groups are all going to clash."

"What do you mean clash?" Frankie said.

"There's going to be a war. I hope I am wrong, but the tensions have been rising awfully quickly."

Frankie didn't know much about war. There hadn't been any wars in her lifetime. There hadn't been any wars in Superion in many, many years. All she knew was that war sounded terrifying.

"But we are all one kingdom," she said. "Why can't everyone get along and work together? Things used to be like that years ago. You taught me that in my history lesson."

"Yes, I wish things could be like that, but unfortunately, things have changed over the years," Thomas said. "Enough of this for now, we have a Traveling lesson to work on."

Frankie took a deep breath and closed her eyes. How was she supposed to Travel? She didn't feel like a Traveler. She didn't feel like much of anything except someone worried about her kingdom. Frankie breathed and focused as much as she could, but like the other day, she didn't go anywhere.

"What's next?" Frankie asked eagerly after lunch. So far, the traditional lessons were much more enjoyable than attempting the Gifts. "Can we have animals again? Or history?"

"Math," Thomas said.

"Okay," Frankie said. Math she could do.

Frankie followed along with the problems Thomas demonstrated. The problems were complicated. Frankie thought it was a little confusing, but she was getting the hang of it. They were only a couple problems in when they were interrupted by someone Traveling into the office. Frankie was used to Travelers, but she jumped in surprise at the intrusion.

"Excuse me! This is a private household! What do you think you're doing?" Thomas demanded as the tiny office became more crowded. "Oh, your Majesties, please forgive me. I'm sorry to shout; you startled me."

Frankie's parents sure were showing up unexpectedly lately. "What are you doing here?" she said. She knew they were the king and queen, but it was rude to just show up in Thomas' house. It was his house, not theirs.

"We came to observe your lesson finally," Queen Veronica said.

"What are you working on?" King Leopold said. They were entirely unapologetic for essentially breaking into Thomas' house.

"Math," Thomas said.

King Leopold scoffed. That wasn't the kind of lesson he wanted to hear about.

"Oh no, we don't want to see a math lesson," Queen Veronica said. "We came here to see a Traveling lesson. Let's see you Travel, Frankie. I bet you're doing wonderfully."

Frankie didn't want to do it. She couldn't Travel even if she wanted to. She looked to Thomas. He was smart and quick; maybe he would come up with an excuse for her.

"We worked on Traveling this morning," Thomas said. "Frankie is still struggling to Travel, which is normal. Many people struggle with their Gifts at first, and we aren't even positive that Frankie's Gift is Travel."

"You have said that before," King Leopold said. He and Queen Veronica sat and made themselves comfortable. "I am tired of hearing all that. I want to see Frankie Travel."

"What do you think, Frankie? Do you want to give it another try?" Thomas asked gently.

No, Frankie didn't want to give it another try, but she didn't have any other choice. Thomas, bless his heart, had tried to get her out of it, but it hadn't worked. Her parents were extremely stubborn. She went back to her corner and closed her eyes. Maybe if she pretended her parents weren't here, she would have better luck, if she was ever going to get lucky at Traveling.

"Where is she trying to go?" King Leopold said.

"The other side of the room," Thomas said.

"In this room?" King Leopold said. "This is like a closet. That is nothing. You are not challenging her."

"It is plenty challenge. Everyone needs to start small," Thomas said patiently.

"Maybe Frankie just needs us for encouragement," Queen Veronica said. "Come on, Frankie. You can do it."

Frankie didn't think that was true. Thomas had told her many, many times that she needed to focus to Travel, or to use any Gift. She was having a hard time focusing when so many people were talking. She did the best she could. It was a very long afternoon. Thomas gave her the usual gentle reminders now and then about breathing and focusing. Her parents grew more frustrated as the afternoon wore on. Even though Frankie kept her eyes firmly shut, she could hear their restless shuffles and sighs. Frankie more than anything wanted to give up for the day, but she didn't dare say so.

"What's wrong with you, Frankie?" King Leopold finally said angrily. "Why aren't you Traveling?"

Frankie opened her eyes. "I'm trying," she said softly. "It's not working. I don't think I'm a Traveler." She could see how disappointed her parents were. Now they had actually witnessed her lack of Traveling.

"Do you think you are a Minder or a Reacher?" Queen Veronica asked, sounding falsely bright.

Frankie shook her head.

"Frankie and I are still in the early stages of working together," Thomas jumped in. "We will find her Gift. Give us time."

"I don't believe you," King Leopold said. "If Frankie has a Gift, she should be demonstrating it by now. My wife and I never had problems using our Gift. We will be back tomorrow morning to see Frankie's Gift, whatever that may be. I wanted a Traveler, but if she is a Minder or a Reacher, that will do. If she cannot show us a Gift, you will be fired as her tutor. Frankie will also no longer be a princess. No one wants a princess who is Not Gifted." With that, the king and queen Traveled from the room.

Frankie had never felt like such a failure, and she was taking Thomas down with her. She couldn't help it; she sat down and cried.

CHAPTER ELEVEN

After she had taken Frankie her lunch, Mena returned to the bakery. Zac trotted along at her side. Even though he had gotten her into trouble, Mena couldn't help but like the dog. She had to admit that it would be much easier to keep him up here where there was no need to hide him. At the rate he was growing, the trick of carrying him around in a bag wouldn't have lasted much longer. She wondered how big he would grow to be.

Mena loved the bakery. She had grown up here. It had been in her family for generations. These days her mother did most of the baking, and her father did most of the waiting on customers and managing the business. Mena didn't have a mind for business, but she loved to bake and cook. She had been helping in the bakery for as long as she could remember, and she had hoped to continue on in the bakery. Unfortunately, that hadn't been reasonable. The bakery hadn't been making enough money for Mena to stay, so she had gone to Superion City in hopes of finding work.

Mena secured Zac in the bakery's backyard before going into the kitchen. The heat slammed into her. It was a drastic change compared to the air conditioning of the castle. Even the castle's kitchen had never felt warm. Mena pushed up the sleeves of her black dress and slipped an apron on. She had a cake to decorate, so she got to work preparing the icing. Cakes were Mena's favorite to make, even if they were a luxury. Most of the bakery customers stuck with hearty breads, but enough bought sweets to justify making them. Mena knew she would have to bring Frankie to the bakery. With Frankie's sweet tooth, she would be in heaven.

"It's time for the meeting," Don announced a few minutes later.

Mena set down the spatula she had been using to smooth the icing. Cake decorating would have to wait for now. Mena didn't want to go to the meeting. The whole thing made her uncomfortable, but seeing as she was already here, she didn't have much of a choice. She had to sit in. She made her way out to the store portion of the bakery. There were about twenty people there. Mena couldn't help but be a little impressed; she hadn't expected so many. All of the chairs at the small tables were taken, so she stood in the back.

"Thank you to Don and Anna for the use of their bakery today," a man said. He stood in front like he was the leader of the meeting; Mena didn't recognize him.

"I see some new faces today. For those of you who don't know me, my name is Mark. I run the clothing factory down the road. Thank you for being here today. It is wonderful to see so many people sympathetic to our cause. We Not Gifted need to unite. It is about time we took back our share of the kingdom."

A young woman at one of the tables spoke up timidly. "I am all for higher wages for the Not Gifted, but things are dangerous out there. If we speak out, the police will take our livelihood from us. They have been killing animals and burning businesses all over the kingdom.

Sometimes the king and queen even do it themselves. How are we ever going to have equality if so much can be taken away from us just for saying something against the way things are in Superion?"

"I know things are scary. That's why we have to join together," Mark said. "We need to unite and start a revolution. A coup is just what this kingdom needs." He paced as he spoke. He was excited and energetic, but he was making Mena nervous. "This royal family has been in power for long enough. All they care about is themselves and their fellow Gifted. They could care less about us. It's about time they were overthrown. We need Not Gifted involved in the leadership of this kingdom once again."

A revolution? A coup? The words terrified Mena. She didn't agree with the king and queen on many things, but they were still Frankie's parents and Mena's employers for now.

"Overthrowing the king and queen sounds well and good, but how do you propose doing that?" a man asked. "Sure, we can attack them, but we won't get far. They are Gifted. All of their police forces are Gifted. We are not. Let's face it; it's a losing battle."

"That's where our numbers come in," Mark said. "They may be able to silence us one by one, but it will be much harder for them to take on all of us at once. Plus, we have allies. Not all Gifted are greedy and selfish. Some are on our side. They will help us."

Many of the people in the room were as excited as Mark now. Not only did they have hope for a revolution, they had a plan. They all started talking at once. It took Mark several minutes to quiet them down.

"Our allies will join us at our next meeting," Mark said. "From there, we can finalize our plan and head to Superion City."

"What about her?" someone asked. To Mena's horror, she realized the woman was pointing at her. She was an older woman who Mena recognized as a frequent customer of the bakery. She had been coming in for years.

"What about me?" Mena asked in a voice that sounded more like a squeak.

"She's Don and Anna's daughter," the woman said. "More importantly, she's the princess's maid. Look at her. If she's here, she's on our side. We have to take advantage of that."

"Is that so?" Mark said. He was downright giddy. "Yes, we have to use her. What's your name, hon?"

"Mena," she managed in a whisper. She didn't even want to be here in the first place, and now she was being singled out.

"Mena, it is lovely to meet you," he said. "Yes, I think you will be a huge help. I hadn't even dreamed of having access to the princess, but we have to use that."

She stood up straight. "No. I won't help you put Princess Frances in danger. She's only a child."

This earned Mena more than a few dirty looks. "More allegiant to them than to her own people," she heard someone mutter.

Mark brushed her off. "Child or not, she is a royal and therefore our enemy." He continued to pace and talked on and on about plans of a revolution. The crowd was enthusiastic. Mena half listened as she thought of how to keep Frankie hidden from these people. They couldn't find out Frankie was here in Aurora Village. At the castle, they had tried to keep Zac hidden; now they had to keep Frankie hidden.

** ** **

Thomas made them tea. Frankie knew she shouldn't cry. She was supposed to act dignified and royal, but she didn't care. By tomorrow, she wouldn't be a royal anyway. She would be an outcast, and then what would she do?

"Drink your tea, Frankie. It will help," Thomas encouraged gently.

Frankie did as she was told. The tea was so hot it burned her throat. She sipped it slowly. "What are we going to do?" she finally asked Thomas.

Before he could answer, there was a knock at the door. Frankie couldn't help feeling frightened. This office had seen a few angry people today; Frankie didn't want to see any more. Thomas motioned for her to stay still. He went to answer the door. She drank her tea and listened as hard as she could.

"I'm here to bring Frankie home," a familiar voice said. Mena. It was Mena; it was a friend.

Frankie couldn't hear what was said next; there was a lot of whispering. Thomas must be telling Mena about the visit from the king and queen. Then Mena and Thomas joined Frankie in the small office. Mena hugged her.

"You poor dear," Mena said soothingly. "You have had a bad day." She looked at the half empty cup of tea in front of Frankie in disapproval. "Don't you have any chocolate?" she asked Thomas.

"I'm sorry, no," he said. "I don't care for chocolate myself."

"How can someone not like chocolate?" Frankie said through her sniffles.

That made Mena smile. She sat down next to Frankie. "What do you want to do?" she said. "Thomas said he can work with you some more, or you can come back with me."

Frankie looked to Thomas. Would he even want to work with her? "It's your decision," he said kindly.

"Then we should work some more," she said. She didn't expect positive results, but she should at least try. It was her last chance to practice. She had thought the Test was a big deal, but showing her parents if she had a Gift was an even bigger test.

"Very well," Thomas said. "You might as well go home and relax, Mena. I'll send Frankie back when she is finished."

"Okay. Please wear this when you walk back," Mena said. She took a cloak and scarf out of her bag and set them on the table. They weren't Frankie's. They looked worn and probably belonged to Mena.

"Thank you, but I don't think I need all that," Frankie said, puzzled. "It's warm out."

"I know, but please wear them," Mena said. "I don't want to alarm you, but there are people who shouldn't see you out and about. Don't worry about it right now. Just concentrate on your lesson, and we'll talk about everything later."

Mena gave Frankie's hand a squeeze before she left. Frankie appreciated the gesture, but she didn't feel comforted. Her parents didn't want her in the castle if she was Not Gifted, and it sounded like she wasn't exactly welcome outside of the castle either.

Thomas sat down across from her. She drank the last of her tea.

"Ready to get back to work?" he said.

She nodded.

They worked on the Minder exercises. With all of the bad news she had received today, focusing was a challenge, but at least she didn't have an audience for this lesson. She closed her eyes and focused on Thomas as best she could. Instead of colors, he used animals because by now, he knew how much Frankie liked animals. Thomas explained that sometimes Minders had to put their own thoughts aside and really listen for someone else's. Frankie tried to do that. To her surprise, she thought she maybe had some success.

"Pig?" she said tentatively.

"No," he said.

"Chicken?" she said.

"No."

"Potato?"

"No."

"Carrot?"

"No. I haven't been thinking any of those things. I was thinking cat. Potatoes and carrots aren't even animals; they're vegetables. Are you hungry, Frankie? We can call it a night if you want to."

"No, I'm okay," Frankie said honestly. It was dinnertime, but she wasn't overly hungry. She didn't know what made her guess foods. She thought she heard Thomas' thoughts but apparently not. "Let's try again," she resolved.

This time Frankie stayed silent. Thoughts crept into her head, but they had to be her own thoughts. They couldn't be Thomas' because they weren't animals.

"I think that's enough of that," Thomas finally said. "Let's try the Reacher exercise for a while."

Frankie opened her eyes. She reached her arms over her head and stretched. She would keep working, but she couldn't help the nagging feeling. "Do you really think I'm Gifted?" she asked.

"I know I keep saying this, but yes, I really do. The Test doesn't lie," Thomas said. "Now stop fretting and concentrate. We may not be successful today, but we're going to give it a try. Okay?"

Frankie nodded. They used the pencil again. Frankie stared at it and willed it to her fingers. She didn't cheat. Her fingers stayed perfectly still on the table. Unfortunately, the pencil stayed still as well. Even though she felt discouraged, Frankie focused with all her might. She focused so hard that when the door opened, she nearly leapt out of her chair.

"Oh, I'm sorry to interrupt," David said. "I didn't know Frankie was still here."

"It's okay," Frankie said. She returned her attention to the pencil in earnest.

"Actually, Frankie, I think it's time to call it a day," Thomas said. "You worked hard today. Now you should go home and rest. Tomorrow is a big day, and rest will help."

"What's tomorrow?" David said.

"If I can't demonstrate a Gift tomorrow, I'm no longer a Princess," Frankie stated.

"Is that so?" David said. "Well, it's a good thing you're Gifted,

Princess."

Frankie managed a weak smile. She knew David was trying to cheer her up. Thomas and Mena would do the same thing. She appreciated it, but she didn't feel cheerful. She had never asked to be a princess, but her life as a princess was the only life she knew. It was hard to be happy when that would most likely be taken away in a matter of hours. She wrapped herself in the cloak and scarf as Mena had instructed. She felt overly warm immediately.

"What's all that for?" David said. "It's summer."

Frankie shrugged. "Mena said I have to wear it."

"David, would you be so kind as to walk Frankie home?" Thomas said.

"It's okay," Frankie said. She toyed with the dark scarf. "I don't mind going by myself. It's not a long walk."

"Really, let David take you," Thomas pressed.

"Yeah, I like to walk. I'll go with you," David said. "Come on, Frankie."

Frankie didn't feel like she needed an escort, but she didn't protest further. She said good night to Thomas and left with David. It was pitch black outside. There were no city lights here. Frankie wondered what time it was. It must be the middle of the night. Realizing the late hour also made her realize how tired and hungry she was. Plus, it was stifling under the cloak. Hot, tired, and hungry wasn't a pleasant combination. She walked quietly next to David. She liked David, but she didn't feel up to conversation at the moment.

"Looks like we're not the only ones out tonight," David said.

A car was traveling toward them. The bright headlights made Frankie blink. She didn't have the energy to wonder where the car was going. She and David were off to the side of the road, so they weren't in danger of being hit. The car slowed as it approached them. That did make her a little nervous.

"What's this about?" David whispered.

Frankie remembered what Mena had said about people seeing her out and about. She adjusted her scarf and edged a bit further from the road. The car came to a complete stop next to them, and the driver had the window rolled down.

"David, I thought that was you," the driver said. It was a man. He sounded friendly enough, but Frankie kept her face hidden. "What are you and your friend doing out so late?"

"She's a patient. I'm walking her home," David said.

"I can give you a ride if you want," the man offered.

"No, thank you. I think some fresh air will do her good," David said.

"Well, you would know. You're the doctor," the man said. "Good night."

"Good night," David replied before the man drove off.

Frankie let out a sigh of relief. If that man had any idea she was the princess, he hadn't let on. If she had to hide from everyone, hiding was going to be a lot of work.

** ** **

Mena sat in the old chair in the parlor and tried to sew. They didn't have a fancy sewing machine here like in the castle, but she could sew by hand. She usually sewed quite well, but not tonight. Tonight she made mistake after mistake. She was only trying to pass the time while she waited for Frankie to come home. It was getting awfully late. Was Frankie going to study all night? That couldn't be good for her. She was young. She needed sleep. Mena set down her sewing project. She had offered to mend an apron for her mother, but with all of the mistakes she was making, she was just making a mess of it. Should she take another walk down to Thomas' house? That would be more productive than sitting here. Then before she could get up from her chair, the door opened.

"Oh, thank goodness you're home," Mena said as a bundled up Frankie walked in. David was behind her.

"Safe and sound," David said. "Good night, ladies."

"Thank you!" Mena said. She gave David a wave before he left. It was good to see him, and she told herself it was only because he had brought Frankie home.

Zac had been napping at Mena's feet, but now that Frankie was home, he was awake. He blinked sleepily and wagged his tail. Frankie pet him before she removed her heavy layers.

"I wouldn't mind all this if it was winter," Frankie said. "Where are your parents? I should say hello to them."

"They're in bed," Mena said.

"Oh, then I can't say hello. I'll see them in the morning."

"Are you hungry?"

"Starving."

The girls went into the kitchen, and Mena heated Frankie's dinner for her. Zac looked hungry, so Mena gave him some roast beef. Mena was quickly learning that growing puppies were always hungry.

As Frankie ate her potato casserole, the girls talked about their eventful day. Frankie told Mena about the visit from her parents and her unsuccessful lessons, and Mena filled Frankie in on the meeting and how some of the townspeople wanted to use Frankie as a tool in their revolution.

"I don't blame them," Frankie said after she had taken the final bite of her potatoes and listened to Mena's story. "They deserve better, but a revolution sounds scary. People will get hurt, Gifted and Not Gifted."

"That's right. That's why we have to keep you hidden," Mena said. "They don't care who gets hurt, and they especially don't care if you get hurt."

Frankie covered her mouth as she yawned. Mena could tell she was exhausted.

"Before we go to bed, I got you a treat," Mena said. "It's not quite as good as hot cocoa, but I think you'll like it."

Mena set the drink and a slice of cake in front of Frankie. Frankie looked at the drink curiously.

"Is it cold cocoa?" she asked.

Mena tried not to giggle. "It's chocolate milk. Try it."

Frankie took a tiny tentative sip. "Hey, that's good."

** ** **

Zac ate his roast beef. Mena always gave him such yummy things to eat. He cuddled up at Frankie's feet. Frankie had been gone for a very long time today, and Zac had missed her. The girls were worried. They kept talking about Frankie and Gifts. Zac wouldn't mind if Frankie didn't have a Gift. He had seen people use their Gifts, and it was scary.

The girls ate cake and drank something new (to Zac and Frankie) called chocolate milk. They let Zac have small bites of cake. Zac loved cake! They didn't let him try the chocolate milk. That was disappointing because Frankie said it was really good, but chocolate was bad for dogs. Instead, Mena gave him a small bowl of white milk. Zac drank it all. He loved milk!

Zac wanted to stay awake with the girls, but he was so tired. He couldn't even walk to their bed when it was time to go. Frankie had to carry him.

CHAPTER TWELVE

"Frankie, wake up."

Frankie woke to Mena and Zac standing over her. Mena was already fully dressed with her hair in a neat bun. Zac looked like he would rather not be awake, and Frankie could sympathize. She was still so tired and didn't want to get out of bed. With dread, she realized what day it was and that sleeping in wasn't an option.

She dressed in the lavender dress that Mena had set out for her and let Mena do her hair. Frankie didn't have much of an appetite, but she ate the oatmeal that Mena made her.

"Mena mentioned that you have a big test today," Anna said pleasantly in an effort to start conversation.

Frankie could only nod.

When it was time to go, Frankie wrapped herself in the dark cloak and scarf. Mena escorted her to Thomas' house. It was a beautiful summer day, but Frankie couldn't pay much attention to her surroundings. She was too busy agonizing over what was about to happen. The Test had been nerve-wracking enough, but this was completely different. She hadn't known what to expect with the Test; she was fairly certain this was going to be a failure.

"There you are!" Queen Veronica exclaimed as they approached the door. While she had almost no optimism about this, Frankie had hoped for some last minute tips from Thomas before her parents arrived. No such luck.

"Good morning, Queen Veronica," Mena said.

"Mena," the queen acknowledged without the hint of a smile. "You had better stay. I think we will need to speak with you as well."

Frankie learned that she was expected to perform a Gift in Thomas' office. Everyone sat in chairs while Frankie stood in the middle of the room. They all expected her to do something, expected her to impress them. Frankie imagined this must be what it felt like for singers and dancers as they stood in front of their audience. The only difference was those people could perform, and Frankie could not perform a Gift.

"Travel," King Leopold said. "To the other side of that window."

Frankie closed her eyes. She couldn't bear them all looking at her. It wasn't a surprise that her father would ask her to Travel first; a Traveler was what her parents wanted most. She focused, but she had no idea how she was supposed to will herself outside. She couldn't even Travel across a room. This was much too hard a challenge. Thomas must certainly agree the king was asking too much, but he was silent. Frankie was silent too. She stood perfectly still, and time passed so very slowly.

"Enough. You are not a Traveler," King Leopold said.

Frankie couldn't agree more, but she kept her mouth shut.

"Reach," King Leopold said. "Take one of the books off the shelf."

Frankie opened her eyes. She studied the bookcases that lined the room. She spotted a book that was much thinner than its neighbors and focused all of her attention on that one little book. If she was going to Reach a book, she might as well try for a small one. As hard as she stared at the little book, it didn't go anywhere. This exercise was just like the Traveling one, entirely unsuccessful.

"You're not a Reacher either," King Leopold declared.

"Please be a Minder, Frankie," Queen Veronica said.

Frankie resisted the urge to roll her eyes. It wasn't like she had a say in the matter.

"Tell me what I'm thinking," Queen Veronica said.

Frankie had no idea where to go with that. Thomas always gave her a category or something. She didn't know how to just listen for thoughts in general, not that she even heard any thoughts anyway. She closed her eyes again. Everyone watching really wasn't helping. What could her mother be thinking? Probably that she was useless and Not Gifted. Frankie did as Thomas had taught her. She relaxed her mind and listened for thoughts.

She heard something! There was a mess of blonde fur. No, that couldn't be what her mother was thinking; she hated animals. Maybe Thomas was thinking cat like last night.

"I'll give you a hint," Queen Veronica finally said. She didn't sound happy. "I'm thinking of a number."

Then she definitely wasn't thinking of blonde fur. Frankie listened as hard as she could. She didn't hear any numbers.

"That's enough," King Leopold said after what felt like an eternity. "You are Not Gifted, Frances. Your title is removed. You are no longer a princess."

Frankie opened her eyes. She wasn't surprised. This was the result she had expected, but it still hurt.

"You may stay with Mena's family if they will have you, or you can go live anywhere in the kingdom you may like," Queen Veronica said. "You're responsible for your own expenses, so I recommend you get a job or find someone to take you in. You're no longer welcome in the castle unless we explicitly invite you. Is that clear?"

Frankie felt the sting of tears but blinked them away. She nodded.

Queen Veronica turned her icy gaze to Mena. "Seeing as you are Frankie's maid, we no longer have use for you. You are a fairly competent maid. I may have kept you on even if that story the driver said was true."

Mena looked as if she was going to say something in reply, but she didn't get a chance. The king and queen Traveled away in an instant.

"I don't even know where to start," Frankie said as they walked back to Mena's house. Had she really been in primary school just a short time ago? So much had changed. She and Mena would both need to get jobs, and it looked like no secondary school for Frankie. Plenty of kids skipped secondary school because they couldn't afford it. Frankie had never thought she would be one of those kids; princesses weren't those kids. There were many things for Frankie to think about, but one basic need had her the most concerned.

"Where am I going to live?"

"With us, of course," Mena said.

"No, that would be too much to ask your family to take me in. Why would you even do that?"

"The same reason you came up here, isn't it? You didn't really come up here for your lessons. You could have just as easily done those at the castle. You came up here for Zac and me. Because we're friends, the three of us, right?"

Frankie adjusted her cloak as she took a moment to think this through. There had been multiple reasons for her to leave the castle, and everything had happened so quickly. But Mena was right. Above all else, she had wanted to stay with her friends; she had been trying to protect them.

"Right," Frankie agreed.

"It's a gift," Mena said. "Friendship is a gift, and some gifts are more valuable than the ones they talk about all the time."

"So friend, now that we are shunned from the castle, what's our first move?"

"Lunch."

Frankie thought that sounded like an excellent idea. She was hungry, and she kind of couldn't believe that it was only lunchtime. That had to have been the longest morning ever.

"What's that?" Mena said.

Frankie followed Mena's gaze to the front door. "It's a dog!"

Frankie left Mena behind and sprinted to the dog. The dog looked up at Frankie hopefully, but she trembled. Frankie crouched down and reached out a hand tentatively.

"It's okay, girl. Can I pet you?"

The dog shook like a leaf but allowed Frankie to pet her. "Hush, you're okay here," Frankie soothed as she petted the thick blonde fur. Despite the thick fur, the dog was very skinny. She didn't have a collar or leash.

Mena hustled, but she wasn't as fast as Frankie. "Where did he come from?" she said when she reached them a moment later.

"She is a girl," Frankie said. "I don't know where she came from. I didn't bring her here."

"No, I know you didn't," Mena said. "Maybe she's lost. In any case, we should bring her in and feed her. The poor thing is fur and bones; she must be hungry."

The girls brought their new friend into the house, and Zac was very interested to meet her. There was a copious amount of sniffing from both dogs. Frankie sat on the floor and played with the dogs while Mena prepared lunch for everyone. Frankie received a shock as she pet the girl dog. She leapt with surprise and let out a cry.

"What's wrong? What happened?" Mena said.

"Her name is Princess," Frankie said. "The woman she belonged to was a cook, Cook Smith. She spoke out and asked for more money, so she was fired. Without work, she became so poor that she was going to cook Princess and eat her. That's why Princess ran away. She stopped here because of Zac. She thought if we had one happy dog, we might like a second one."

"Princess – the dog – thought all that?" Mena said in disbelief. "How do you know?"

"I heard her. I don't know how. I just did." Frankie knew it sounded crazy.

Mena had to abandon the lunch preparations and sit down. "Like you're a Minder?"

"But I'm not a Minder. I could never hear Thomas during our lessons, and I couldn't hear my mother today. If I was a Minder, don't you think it would have come out by now?"

Mena looked thoughtful. "You can't hear people. Maybe you're a Minder who can hear animals. Your Test said you had a different Gift."

"Maybe," Frankie said. Even though Thomas had told her countless times that she was Gifted and they would figure it out, she had had her doubts. She had thought it more likely that she was Not Gifted. It was hard to think that Thomas really could have been right all along.

"Let's go back to Thomas'. We can ask him about it."

"No, not yet. Maybe I dreamt all that about Princess. Let me practice for a while."

"That's a lot to dream up, but okay," Mena said. "I will get our lunch."

Mena went back to making lunch, and Frankie stayed with the dogs. How was she supposed to practice this potential Gift? Thomas had taught her the first lesson of Minding; she guessed it was similar. She reached for Zac and started petting his black fur.

"Zac, tell me something. What's your favorite food?" she said.

Frankie kept petting as she focused. Almost in an instant, cake and milk popped into her head. She saw it from Zac's perspective. He sat on the floor between Mena and Frankie as Mena poured him a bowl of milk.

"Cake and milk," Frankie said with confidence. It was not at all a guess.

Zac wagged his tail. Then more images flooded Frankie's mind. The day she had yelled at the mean old man to leave Zac alone and then taken him away. Playing with the teddy bear. Playing in the grass around the castle while Mena picked flowers. Cuddling up in Frankie's bed. She saw it all from Zac's eyes. She saw how she and Mena looked to him. He adored them.

"I love you too, Zac," Frankie said. She gave him a big hug. "I want to hear Princess now."

Frankie pet the girl dog. "Same question, Princess. What's your favorite food?"

At first, Frankie couldn't hear anything. She focused, and an image finally came to her mind. It was of a bowl like Zac's, but it was empty.

"Oh Princess, I know you're hungry. We will feed you, but tell me, what do you like to eat? You have to have eaten sometime. Cook Smith must have fed you."

Princess told Frankie about the cook. She wasn't always a bad person. Princess used to sit in the kitchen with her as she cooked and cooked. Princess showed Frankie what seemed like an endless parade of food, all of the different things the cook used to make. Ham came up a lot, so Frankie guessed that was Princess' favorite. Then Princess remembered how desperate the cook had become, and she became very frightened.

"It's okay, Princess. You're safe with us," Frankie soothed. "And you're in luck. Mena has ham for you and Zac."

Frankie kept petting the dogs. As she sat quietly, the dogs sent her more thoughts. They weren't stories. They were random images like soft blankets and cold water. Frankie also got that the dogs liked it here. They didn't have to be afraid here.

"Lunch," Mena announced.

Frankie already knew the dogs were grateful for their lunch. She joined Mena at the table.

"You heard them, right?" Mena said.

"Yes," Frankie said between bites of cheese sandwich. "I wish you could hear them too. It's amazing."

"I am not Gifted. You are. I always knew you were," Mena said. "And I guess we have two dogs now. We can't send her back to someone who wants to cook her."

"We have to keep her," Frankie said. She had always liked animals and wanted a dog; she hadn't expected two to find her.

"We have to give her a new name though. I don't think I can call a dog Princess."

"Why not? I'm not a Princess anymore. One of us can be called Princess, just not me."

Mena shook her head. "It's just not right."

"Fine, you can name her then. I got to name Zac."

Mena set down her sandwich and thought this over. Giving a dog a name was a big responsibility. "Let's call her Foxy."

"Foxy? Do you like that?" Frankie asked the girl dog.

She told Frankie that she did indeed like her new name. She liked to run fast like foxes. She even wagged her tail to show Mena she was happy.

"I wonder what Thomas will think of this," Frankie said as she, Mena, and the dogs set out on their walk. She was once again concealed in her warm disguise, and she held Zac's leash. Mena held Foxy's leash; Mena had fashioned a simple collar and leash for Foxy out of rope.

"It's a surprise, that's for sure, but we knew you were special," Mena said.

"I'm different. That doesn't make me special," Frankie said. "Foxy likes this. The cook hadn't taken her for a walk in a long time."

"I'm glad she found us," Mena said. "I'm sorry you have to wear such a boring collar, Foxy. I'll make you a pretty pink one soon."

"She likes that. Pink is her favorite color," Frankie translated.

Despite the fact that she was sweltering in the cloak, Frankie enjoyed their walk. She touched minds with the dogs the whole time. While most humans liked their thoughts to remain private, Zac and Foxy didn't have those reservations. They were excited to share with Frankie all of the neat things they saw on the walk. – There's a squirrel! Look at those pretty flowers! – Frankie was still getting used to thinking of herself as Gifted, and she couldn't believe her luck in having such an amazing Gift. If she had dared hope for some mysterious never before seen Gift, this was definitely the Gift she would have hoped for.

She already loved her Gift, and she couldn't wait for Thomas to instruct her so that she could use it fully. When they reached his house, she knocked on the door with enthusiasm.

It only took him a moment to answer the door. "What are you girls doing here?" he said. "It's not that I'm unhappy to see you, but I was just on my way out."

Frankie noticed his heavy bookbag over his shoulder. "Do you have a lesson?" she said. She knew teaching was his job, but had she really been replaced as a pupil so quickly?

"Yes, I'm on my way to work with a Reacher," Thomas said. "I had been working with him for quite a while, but I had to put our lessons on hold when your parents called me, Frankie. One does not turn down a request from the king and queen. I don't mean to sound disrespectful, but they aren't people who will take no for an answer."

"Oh," was all Frankie could say. She had liked working with Thomas very much, but she didn't like the idea that she had pulled him away from another student. He was right about her parents. They were certainly pushy.

"I don't want to keep you, but we have something to tell you," Mena said. "Can we come in for a minute?"

"I'm afraid now is not a good time," Thomas said. "I must be on my way. Why don't you come over tonight to watch the mandatory viewing? A bulletin went out a few minutes ago that the king and queen have urgent news they want to share with the kingdom. I hate to say it,

Frankie, but I think the news is about you."

** ** **

"What do you want to do?" Mena asked as they walked. They were headed back toward her house, but she wasn't sure if that was where they were going. It was strange not to have anywhere she was expected to be.

"Well, we will have to find jobs," Frankie said. "I can't even go to secondary school or hire a tutor until I have money, but let's not worry about that yet. We will look for jobs tomorrow, if I can even find a job. My parents will probably tell the kingdom awful things about me on television tonight, and after that, who's going to hire me? Until then, let's have summer vacation, just for today."

Mena knew she needed to find work, but Frankie was right. What was the harm in putting that off for just one day? "That sounds perfect," she said. "Let's have a little fun. I heard the kids in Superion City like to go to the swimming pools in the summertime. I'm afraid we don't have any swimming pools around here, but I can think of the perfect place to take you. You'll love it."

Mena led the way to the bakery. They were almost there when she saw the woman. She tensed. It had been bad enough when this woman had pointed Mena out at the meeting, telling the crowd that she was Frankie's maid and vital to the revolution. She couldn't let this woman see Frankie, princess or not.

Mena pointed to the bakery and handed Foxy's leash to Frankie. "The bakery is that building. Run ahead with the dogs. I will meet you around back," she said in a hurried whisper.

Fortunately, Frankie didn't ask questions. She and the dogs took off. Running wasn't ladylike, but now Mena was glad Frankie had never

110

paid attention to that rule. She was fast.

As if on cue, the woman asked Mena "Who was that?"

"A cousin. She is here on her summer vacation," Mena said smoothly. She had the fib ready; she knew someone was bound to ask sooner or later.

"Why is she dressed like that? She knows it's summer, doesn't she?"

"She is from the south. Our heat actually seems cold to her. Now if you will excuse me, I really must go. That girl is always getting into trouble. I can't let her out of my sight for more than a minute."

The woman looked like she still had a litany of questions, but Mena hustled to the bakery before she could ask any more. She unlocked the kitchen door for Frankie.

"You can go in. I'll be right there," Mena said. She secured the dogs in the yard. The dogs wouldn't have much room to run around, but they would be more comfortable out here than in the hot kitchen. When she went inside, she found Frankie had already removed her cloak and scarf and was rolling up the sleeves of her dress.

"I'm sorry," Frankie said. "It's so warm. You don't think I need to be disguised in here, do you?"

"It's okay, we should be safe here," Mena said. "And it is warm." She pushed open the windows; it helped slightly. "You have such a sweet tooth; I thought it would be fun for you to learn how to bake."

Frankie's face broke into a huge grin. "Really?"

"Yes, really," Mena knew the royals rarely went in the kitchen at the castle, let alone cooked or baked anything. The king and queen thought they were above it, and everyone thought Frankie would only get in the way. Mena took two aprons out of a drawer and handed one to Frankie.

"Wow, I feel like a baker already," Frankie said as she tied on her apron.

Mena smiled. She knew Frankie didn't care about such things, but it would be a shame to get her pretty dress dirty. Dirtier than it was anyway. She had managed to get the hem a bit muddy on the walk outside.

Mena decided they would make oatmeal cookies. Those were always a good seller. First, she gathered their ingredients. Frankie just watched; she didn't know what the ingredients were or where they were kept. Mena let Frankie help measure and mix. Then Mena showed her how to scoop spoonfuls of cookie dough onto the baking sheet. Frankie liked that part. It was probably the first time she was actually encouraged to get her hands dirty. Mena put the first sheets into the oven.

Satisfied that Frankie could scoop out dough on her own, Mena turned her attention to a cake that her mother had left for her to decorate. As she prepared the frosting, she tried not to worry. She knew there was nothing wrong with relaxing for a few hours, but she couldn't help but wonder what was going to happen to the two of them. Frankie may have been stripped of her title, but she was Gifted. She would be fine. Mena would join the unemployed, which was quite a large group for the Not Gifted. She sighed. It didn't help anything to worry.

"Mena, look out!" Frankie shouted.

In horror, Mena jumped back from the counter. A small fire had burst up next to the cake she was about to decorate. Frankie ran to the sink and filled a mixing bowl with water. She threw the water on the fire. It took a few more bowls of water, but the girls quickly extinguished the flames. The dogs barked outside.

"What happened? Did it come from the oven?" Frankie said.

"No, it couldn't have. The oven is all the way over there," Mena said. As she said it, she stared at the oven on the other side of the room. The fire coming from the oven really was impossible. She poked around on the counter, looking for a cause. She knew she hadn't started the fire. She had been working with frosting, and it wasn't like frosting could set itself on fire. "I have no idea where it came from," she finally said.

"The window is open. Could someone have thrown something in here?" Frankie suggested.

"I guess it's possible, but there should be a match or something," Mena said, entirely puzzled. The whole thing was a mystery, a troubling mystery. They were lucky they hadn't been hurt. "Better take those cookies out of the oven," she said. "We don't want anything else to burn in here."

** ** **

Zac wagged his tail when Frankie and Mena emerged from the bakery.

"Want a cookie?" Frankie asked.

Yes, he told her. He loved that he could think things and show her things, and Frankie would hear him.

"The bakery will sell the cookies we made, but Mena said we could eat a few."

The cookie was delicious. Frankie and Mena were good at baking. He and Foxy had liked sitting outside the bakery. The grass was soft and comfy, but then there had been a fire in the bakery, and that had been very scary. What if something had happened to the girls? He didn't want the girls to get hurt, and what would happen to the dogs if something happened to the girls? He and Foxy had barked for help.

"Zac, there was a fire today," Frankie said. She sat down in the grass next to him.

Zac showed her how frightened he had been.

"Do you know how it started? Was there anyone outside?"

No, Zac said. He showed her the empty yard. Zac and Foxy wouldn't have let anyone try to hurt the girls anyway. If anyone had come into the yard, Zac and Foxy would have chased them away.

CHAPTER THIRTEEN

Thomas' living room was crowded as they waited for the mandatory viewing to start. It was good that Thomas had invited them. Since Mena's family didn't have a television, they had to go over someone's house to watch the program. Frankie would prefer not to watch this at all, but if she did have to watch it, she would rather be surrounded by friends than by strangers. She and Mena sat on the floor close to the television, while Thomas, David, Don, and Anna sat on chairs behind them. Frankie had always hated when her parents paraded her on mandatory viewing like a puppet. This was even worse. She was so nervous, but nervous as she was, she hoped the program would hurry up and start. They might as well get it over with.

Finally, the king and queen appeared on the screen. They wore formal attire and their crowns. They must mean business if they broke out the crowns. They almost never wore their crowns. Really, who wore a crown? It was quite impractical and uncomfortable. Frankie used to wear her mother's crown when she was little and played dress-up. It was so heavy. Frankie's tiara was light and cute, but she rarely wore it. Impractical.

"Good evening," King Leopold said. "Queen Veronica and I would like to address what we see to be a very problematic trend – the recent actions of the Not Gifted. There seems to be a false belief of equality spreading throughout Superion. Superion is a kingdom built on inequality. The Gifted and Not Gifted are not equal. In order for our society to function, the Not Gifted must remain below the Gifted. We don't take these rumblings lightly. Any act of rebellion against the kingdom will be punishable by death."

Now it was Queen Veronica's turn to speak. "King Leopold and I take this matter quite seriously," she said. "As you know, this kingdom has long been ruled by the Gifted. My husband and I recently had the horror of learning that our own daughter is Not Gifted. As such, she has been stripped of her title. She is an extremely dangerous individual. Look at what she did to this innocent young man."

Adam was brought to stand next to the queen. He had a purple bruise where Frankie had punched him. He stared into the camera smugly. Ugh, what a jerk.

"A Gifted person would not have resorted to such ugly violence," the queen continued. "Frances is dead to us. We have no use for such a disappointment of a daughter. If you should see her in the kingdom, we recommend you stay away from her. Look at what she is capable of. King Leopold and I will discuss the issue of an heir at a later time."

The king and queen bid good night to the kingdom, and Frankie felt Mena's arms go around her.

"That was awful," Mena whispered into Frankie's hair.

Frankie felt numb. She could understand being stripped of her title, but how could she be dead to them? They were her parents. How could they forget about her so easily? The fact that she actually was Gifted didn't seem to help matters. Her parents hated animals. They would think her Gift useless, not that she could tell them about it anyway.

Frankie only half heard the encouragements of everyone around her. They still loved her, princess or not. She was grateful for her small circle of friends, but she couldn't help feeling overwhelmed by the whole experience.

"Why don't we tell Thomas your news?" Mena suggested.

"Yes, what is it?" Thomas said. "I would love to hear it. I'm sorry I couldn't hear it earlier."

"Actually, could you talk later?" Anna said. "We really should get the girls home."

Frankie knew she should tell Thomas about her Gift, but she didn't feel up to protesting. She could tell him tomorrow. Mena bundled her up in the disguise, but Frankie doubted the disguise was necessary anymore. How could anyone want to use her for her power? She was no longer a princess, and the whole kingdom knew it. She had no power.

** ** **

Mena helped her mother make tea for everyone. She wished they had hot cocoa. If Frankie had ever needed a mug of hot cocoa for comfort, it was now, but tea would have to do. Mena set out cookies as well.

Mena sat at the kitchen table with her parents and Frankie. They all drank tea and ate cookies, but it was quiet. No one knew what to say. There was only so much they could say to try to cheer Frankie up, and Frankie didn't appear cheered. Mena didn't blame her. Mena's own family wasn't rich or powerful, but they stuck together. Mena didn't have to worry about her parents saying she was dead to them.

"Frankie, you know we're sorry for the news you have received today," Anna said. "But Mena, we have some news for you as well. We probably should have told you this a long time ago, but we didn't know how." She set her teacup down nervously. "I guess we were waiting for the perfect moment, and now is as good a time as any. I'm still not sure how to say this, but you are not our daughter."

"What?" Mena gasped, almost choking on her tea. That was the last thing she had expected to hear.

"Of course you are our daughter," Don said. "We didn't mean it like that."

"Yes, of course," Anna said. "You are our daughter, and we love you. What I mean to say is you're adopted. Your real parents are the king and queen."

"Mena and I are sisters?" Frankie said excitedly. Something had finally cheered her up.

"Well, yes," Anna said. "You see, there is a test they can give babies to see if the girls and boys will grow up to be Gifted or not. It's not nearly as accurate as the test they give you when you're fourteen. Not many people bother with the baby test. Let the child grow up some before worrying about Gifts.

"Given the prejudices of the king and queen, you can see why they would want their baby tested. When your baby test turned out to be Not Gifted, they said they didn't want you anymore. They talked about having you killed, but cold hearted as they are, I don't think even they could kill their own baby.

"Helen worked in the castle as a maid then. She said 'I know a couple way up in the north who want a baby more than anything. They will raise this baby girl as if she is their own.' Helen was very brave to speak up like she did, and you were brought to us. No one in the kingdom was to know.

"Now, the whole kingdom had seen the queen's pregnant belly. When there was no baby, people became curious. There was mandatory viewing, just as there was tonight, and it was announced that the baby had died. People were forbidden to talk about it. Frankie was born a few years later, and the supposed deceased baby was completely forgotten."

Mena couldn't believe it. "I could have been a princess," she breathed. She couldn't help but give a fleeting thought to the idea that she could have grown up in the castle.

"Yes, and maybe if you had worked with someone like Thomas, you could have developed your Gift. We will never know," Anna said. "I have to admit I'm glad you weren't a princess. If you were, we wouldn't have had a daughter."

"I have had a blessed life," Mena said resolutely. "And I don't think lessons with a tutor would have helped me. I am Not Gifted."

"That's not what your Test result was," Anna said.

"What was your Test result?" Frankie said. "You told me you were Not Gifted."

"I am Not Gifted," Mena said. "But my Test result was the same as yours. It was inconclusive."

"I have a Gift," Frankie said. "You probably do too. We have to tell Thomas about this when we see him tomorrow. We can tell him. He can keep a secret."

"Frankie, what do you mean you have a Gift?" Anna said. "The king and queen just stood in front of the whole kingdom and said you were Not Gifted."

"I have a Gift they don't know about yet. I can hear the thoughts of animals," Frankie said. Mena's parents stared at her. Frankie ignored them. "Come on, Mena. You must be Gifted too."

"No, I'm not," Mena protested. "I have tried. I have tried to Mind, Reach, and Travel but with no success. We could never afford a tutor like Thomas, but even without a tutor, I should have shown some Gift on my own by now. I tried for years. When you could hear Zac and Foxy today, I even tried to do that, but it didn't work. I really am Not Gifted."

"Are you angry with us?" Anna said.

Mena took a moment to think this through. "No," she decided. "I don't want to talk about Gifts because I believe I am Not Gifted, and I have accepted that. I'm glad you told me about my family. As far as I'm concerned though, you're my parents, not the king and queen who thought about having me killed. The biggest blessing is that Frankie is my sister. I long ago gave up on any hope of siblings. Frankie has been a dear friend to me, even if she does have a knack for trouble."

Today was a whirlwind, Mena reflected as she climbed into bed. She knew it would be a day of revelation for Frankie; she hadn't expected it to be so revealing for herself. She didn't mind that she wasn't raised a princess. Her life here wasn't glamorous, but it was a good life. Frankie was her sister. There couldn't be a better surprise than that. Frankie often felt more like a friend than a charge child to look after; that must be why. Mena was lucky to have such a sister.

Frankie and Zac were already sound asleep in their bed on the floor. Foxy would sleep in Mena's bed. Frankie insisted that Mena needed a bed dog too, although Mena suspected Frankie would have gladly let both dogs sleep in her bed. Mena never had a bed dog before. Heck, they had only been looking after Zac for a short time. Mena took a sip of water from the glass on the nightstand. Then she snuggled next to Foxy. Foxy had told Frankie she liked it here. Mena hoped that was true; no dog deserved to suffer. Foxy was very soft, and judging by her deep breathing, Mena guessed she was already asleep. Mena would like having a bed dog. It was like having a teddy bear, only a living and breathing one.

Mena's thoughts finally quieted down, and she drifted off to sleep. It was a fitful sleep as she dreamt. She dreamt she was in the castle, in a car, at the bakery. Then she dreamt she was in a strange place full of fire.

** ** **

Zac woke up with a start and a bark. Something wasn't right. Frankie was still asleep; she was safe. Then Zac saw it. None of them were safe. A fire smoldered on the nightstand. Zac barked and barked. The others started to stir. Then he spotted the glass of water on the nightstand. He remembered the girls talking about how they had used water to put out the fire at the bakery. Zac jumped up and knocked the glass over. He was still a growing puppy. He was barely tall enough, but he did it. Zac kept them safe.

CHAPTER FOURTEEN

"You don't have to dress me, you know," Frankie said when she saw the dress Mena had set out for her.

"I'm not your maid anymore, but I am your big sister," Mena said as she pinned her fair hair up in a bun. "I can dress you if I want. Besides, if I left it up to you, you would probably wear pajamas all day, and that's not at all appropriate for job hunting."

Frankie had to admit Mena was probably right. She dressed in the plain black dress. She liked it, but she didn't remember it. Her dresses tended to be more colorful. "Is this yours?" she asked Mena.

"It used to be. It looks like it's yours now. It was a little short on me anyway. You should probably share my dresses until we can get you some new ones. Maybe this will be a better disguise for you than that heavy cloak. Pretty as they are, your royal dresses will make you stand out. It's best if you blend in. Princess or not, there are likely still people who want to use you against the king and queen."

122

Frankie didn't mind changing her wardrobe to blend in. She had never been interested in fancy dresses anyway.

Mena waited with the hairbrush. "Would you like me to put your hair up?"

"Okay," Frankie said. She obediently sat on the edge of the bed. If they were altering her appearance, she could think of something else she wanted to try.

"Will you cut my hair?"

"You have such beautiful hair. I don't want to cut it," Mena protested.

"I never liked it long. And, everyone knows the princess with long hair. It can be part of my new look."

With a sigh, Mena got her sewing scissors. "I hope you don't regret this," she said as she started to cut.

"It will always grow back," Frankie said. She watched chunks of dark hair fall to the floor. Zac sniffed at it curiously. Mena marched her in front of the mirror. Frankie stared at her reflection. Mission accomplished. Between the dress and the hair, she no longer looked like a princess. She looked like a regular girl. Mena did a nice job. Frankie's dark hair fell to right above her shoulder.

"I like it," Frankie said.

"Are you sure?" Mena asked hesitantly. "It looks nice on you, but I liked it better long."

"I'm positive. It's perfect."

The girls and dogs made their way to the kitchen. Mena's parents were shocked by Frankie's appearance. Frankie said she was trying to not look so royal. Frankie insisted Mena let her help prepare breakfast. She ate breakfast every day, and she had no idea how to make it. Now that she wasn't a princess anymore, she should learn how to do practical things like feed herself. Mena showed her how to boil water for oatmeal.

"You don't even know how to boil water?" Don said incredulously.

Frankie wasn't sure if he meant it to be offensive. She shrugged. "Yesterday at the bakery was the first time I was allowed in a kitchen. I went in the kitchen at the castle now and then, but that was only when I snuck in to look for treats."

"You can't blame her," Anna said. "She was brought up a royal, and royals have a completely different lifestyle than us."

It would probably be mundane to most people, but Frankie thought it was neat to watch the oatmeal cook. It was interesting to see how one of her favorite foods was made. When it was finished, Mena let her sprinkle just the right amount of cinnamon.

"So, are you girls hoping to find jobs today?" Don asked when they were all sitting down with their oatmeal.

"Hoping," Mena said.

Frankie tried to take a bite of oatmeal, but it was too hot. She blew on it. "Could we work at the bakery?" she said. "I liked baking cookies yesterday. That was fun."

Anna shook her head. "I'm afraid that won't work, hon. We're barely getting by at the bakery as it is. It's just not bringing in enough money."

Don folded up the newspaper he had been reading. "What about the clothing factory? Someone mentioned they were looking for girls to work there. Mena already knows how to sew, and Frankie could learn."

"I could, and everyone needs clothes," Frankie said. A job at the clothing factory sounded perfectly reasonable.

Mena looked concerned. "Doesn't Mark run the clothing factory?"

"Yes, and he's a very nice man," Don said.

Mena stared down at her oatmeal. "No, that won't work. He was rather enthusiastic about using me to get to the royal family. I couldn't trust him."

"What about the woman who owns the sheep farm?" Anna said. "She was in the bakery the other day. She's getting up in years and can't do as much on her own. She said she could use someone to help her."

Mena looked more hopeful at that. "That's a possibility."

"I like sheep," Frankie said.

"Can you really hear the thoughts of animals?" Don said.

Frankie nodded. "I can. I have only been able to practice with Zac and Foxy so far. It will be fun to practice with the sheep. Actually, Zac is speaking to me right now. He really has to go to the bathroom. Excuse me. I should let them out."

The woman who owned the sheep farm was named Betty. Despite her gray hair, she seemed youthful. She was pleasant enough, and if she knew Frankie was the former princess, she didn't let on.

"I don't know that I have enough work for the two of you, but we can see how it goes," Betty said. "One of you can help me spin the wool inside, and the other can stay outside and mind the sheep."

"My sister is great with animals," Mena said. "She would probably like to stay outside. Wouldn't you, Frankie?"

"Oh, yes," Frankie said.

Betty looked at her curiously. "What did you say your name was?"

"Frances, but my friends call me Frankie."

"Frances is a nice name. It reminds me of that poor girl who used to be our princess. Did you see that on television last night? It's a shame what her parents did to her. She can't help what she is. Then again, who am I to judge the king and queen?" Betty shook her head sadly.

Frankie appreciated the sympathy from a stranger. Betty handed her a staff and gave her some advice before leaving her alone with the sheep. It was basically don't let the sheep wander off. Frankie thought she could handle it.

Mena went inside with Betty to spin wool. That sounded interesting, but Frankie would rather stay with the sheep. She gazed at the fence at the edge of Betty's property as she twirled the staff in her hand. She wondered how the sheep could possibly wander past a fence. She also wondered what the staff was for. Betty hadn't explained those things. Oh well, Frankie would do what she was told. She needed the job.

Almost like she was back in a lesson with Thomas, Frankie forced herself to breathe and focus. She didn't close her eyes though. What if one of the sheep ambled away while she had her eyes closed? That would be no good. She listened for the sheep closest to her. It took a minute, but she could hear him.

Betty takes care of me. I love Betty. Where is Betty? Who is this new girl taking care of me? Well, I might as well graze. I love grass.

Frankie tried this with more of the sheep. If they had any idea she could listen to them, they didn't seem to mind. They just went about their business. Much of their thoughts were the same. They loved Betty, and they loved grass. Some wondered who Frankie was and what she was doing there. Some admired the flowers in the garden. Some got frightened when cars drove down the nearby road; cars were loud and scary.

Frankie remembered that some Minders could project their thoughts to others. She wasn't a typical Minder, but maybe she could do something similar. If she could hear the thoughts of the animals, could she will them to hear her? Frankie hadn't tried it with the dogs yet, but she might as well try it with the sheep. She would be here with them all day anyway.

She wasn't sure how to go about it, so she thought as loud as she could toward the sheep. *My name is Frankie, and I am here to help Betty take care of all you nice sheep.*

Frankie, some of them repeated. It was working! The sheep could hear her.

Frankie talked to the sheep all day. She told them not to wander off, but the sheep were happy here. They didn't want to leave. She told them about her dogs and about the city. Some listened to her stories, but others were content to just meander around and graze. She was very careful not to think of the last sheep she had seen, the sheep that had been slaughtered by the king and queen.

Since Frankie still wasn't sure what the staff was for, she asked the sheep about it. The sheep showed her images of cars and monsters leaping over the fence with Betty beating them away with the staff. Frankie wasn't sure if that was true, but if the staff made the sheep feel more safe, she would hold onto it.

With the sheep to talk to, the day passed quickly. Nevertheless, she looked forward to going home to play with the dogs. Mena should be out soon, and they would go home. Some of the sheep noticed the stranger on the road before Frankie did.

Frankie, what's that man doing? I never saw him before, a fuzzy little sheep said.

He's probably just going for a walk, Frankie said.

Then the man stopped at the fence. "Hello, young lady. Where's Betty?"

Beat him with the staff, Frankie! one of the sheep said.

Hush, we'll be alright, Frankie said to calm the sheep. She didn't think beating this man would be necessary, but she did grip the staff a little tighter.

"Betty's inside," she said to the man. She wasn't sure what to do. She felt rude standing there, but if she went inside to get Betty, she would be leaving the sheep with a stranger. She doubted he wanted to steal or hurt the sheep, but she probably shouldn't take chances. It was her first day on the job.

She glanced up at the house. Betty and Mena were coming out now. That was perfect timing! Frankie was so relieved.

"Who's there?" Betty called.

"Hello Betty. My name is Mark. I run the clothing factory," he said.

"I have heard about you," Betty said. She had been perfectly friendly toward Mena and Frankie, but she wasn't friendly now. Whatever she had heard about Mark hadn't been pleasant. Then Frankie remembered that she had heard about Mark too.

"I was hoping you would come to the meeting tonight," Mark said. "We need as many people as we can get. We Not Gifted need to stick together. We all heard what the king and queen said last night. Now more than ever is the time for a revolution."

Betty didn't look impressed by Mark's speech.

"Oh, I know you," he said as he spotted Mena. "Mena, right?"

Mena nodded, but her cold expression matched Betty's.

"You were the princess's maid. No more princess. That would explain what you're doing up here, hanging around the sheep farm and the bakery instead of the castle," Mark said. He turned to get a better look at Frankie. "I thought this pretty girl looked familiar. Looks like we found where the princess is hiding."

Frankie glared at him. Mena was smart, and if Mena didn't trust this man, neither did she.

"The girl who was disowned by her royal parents all because she is Not Gifted. Think of the potential. You could be the poster child of our revolution," Mark said. "You can't go around beating people up though, hon. Try for sweet and innocent. That will give us a better rallying point. You definitely have to come to the meeting tonight. We can use all the Not Gifted we can get, but we can especially use you."

"What if I'm not interested?" Frankie said. She stood up tall and tried to look fierce. She didn't like what Mark had to say; she didn't feel like acting sweet.

"No one is forcing you to come, but I hope you will," Mark said. "I can't say we'll keep that attitude in the future though. Desperate times call for desperate measures. I do hope to see all of you tonight. Your father is so very generous to let us meet at the bakery, Mena. Well, I must be on my way. I have lots of visits to make. See you."

CHAPTER FIFTEEN

Frankie sank into a chair at the kitchen table. Zac and Foxy bounced around, so happy to have Frankie and Mena back home. Frankie rubbed her head; she had a headache ever since the encounter with Mark.

"I don't want to go to that meeting," Frankie whined.

"Neither do I," Mena said softly as she leaned against the counter. "I don't like any of it. I just want to be left alone and make an honest living. I don't want to be involved in a revolution."

Frankie pushed her short hair back off her face. "I agree that the Not Gifted deserve equality, but I don't think Mark and his friends care who gets hurt. That's not right."

Mena started to take vegetables out of the refrigerator. She was getting ready to prepare dinner.

"Do you want help?" Frankie offered. She knew how to make

oatmeal now; maybe she could add another dish to her repertoire.

"No, that's okay," Mena said. "Could you take the dogs out though? Don't go too far. Just stay out back, alright?"

Frankie got the leashes. Zac and Foxy were very excited to go outside. They didn't even seem to mind that they only paced back and forth in the yard.

"I minded sheep today," Frankie said. "Maybe I can show you."

Frankie focused. If she could hear both sheep and dogs, she should be able to project to both sheep and dogs. She thought about the sheep she had spent the day with.

Ooh, sheep! Foxy said.

Frankie smiled. It was working. She showed Zac and Foxy the soft fuzzy wool and how the sheep loved to eat grass. She showed how some of the sheep stayed close to her and safe, while others were more adventurous and wandered closer to the edge of Betty's property.

Sheep are fuzzy and cute! Zac said.

Frankie was glad it had worked. She liked to talk to the dogs, but now she could actually show them things.

Frankie, we need to show you what happened today, Zac said.

Okay, what is it? Frankie said.

Zac was asleep in the living room. Something woke him up. There was a sound at the front door. He and Foxy jumped up and ran to the door. They didn't know who was out there. Whoever it was didn't smell familiar. The stranger was on the move and circling the house. Zac and Foxy were on the move too. They finally met the stranger in the kitchen.

He stared in the window at them. Zac showed Frankie the man's face.

Frankie gasped.

What is it, Frankie? Zac said. *Is he a bad man?*

Probably, Frankie said. *I saw him today too.* She showed the dogs her own encounter with Mark. She told them as much of the conversation as she could remember.

He seems mean, Foxy said.

What about after he saw you in the window? Frankie said.

Nothing, Zac said. *He just left.*

What do you think he wanted, Frankie? Foxy said.

Frankie considered this as they paced. *I don't know, but we should tell Mena about it.*

Once inside, Frankie told Mena the dogs' story. "What do you think he was looking for?"

"He was probably looking for me. I bet he wanted to try to recruit me for this meeting," Mena said. She took the roasted vegetables out of the oven. They smelled delicious.

Frankie set out the knives and forks. She was allowed to set the table. Mena had given her that chore. Mena's explanation made sense, but something still didn't quite add up.

"What about the part of looking in the windows?" Frankie said. "If you knock on someone's door and they're not there, you leave. You don't go and snoop around. It's weird."

"Yes, it is, but I don't think Mark cares about being nosy," Mena said as she scooped vegetables onto plates. "Anyway, let's not worry about it. We have jobs now, and that's something to celebrate."

"I know, but I am worried," Frankie said as she helped set the plates on the table. "I should go to the meeting tonight."

"I thought you didn't want to," Mena said.

Frankie pulled out a chair and sat down. "I don't, but if he wants to snoop around our house and use me as his poster child, I want to see what he is up to."

Mena sighed. The front door opened. "Don't tell my parents about any of this. They think Mark is very nice. They won't believe us that he is very not."

** ** **

Mena sipped her tea nervously. She didn't want to be here. She just wanted to mind her own business, but Frankie insisted on being here. Mena may not have a princess to look after anymore, but she did have a little sister to look after.

"May we join you?" someone asked.

Mena was wound so tight that she almost jumped, but then she saw friendly faces. She hadn't been expecting that. It was Thomas and David.

"Of course," Frankie said. "But what are you doing here? I thought this meeting was for the Not Gifted."

"Gifted allies," Thomas said as he and David sat down at the tiny table. His tone was friendly enough, but Mena thought he and David looked as nervous as she felt. David gave her a smile. Mena tried to smile back without blushing.

"Thank you all for being here this evening," Mark said, bringing the meeting to order. The bakery was crowded, but all of the chatter abruptly stopped. "Thank you especially to the Gifted allies who are joining us. Your support is much appreciated, and it will be crucial to our success. I know everyone here heard the king and queen's comments last night. It was mandatory. It was mandatory for half the kingdom to know they are thought of as less than human. The king and queen have made their stance known. Now we are going to make our stance known. We demand equality. We leave in two days. Contingents from four directions will attack Superion Castle, attack them from every side. We are part of the northern contingent. We have weapons, and we have our Gifted allies to help us. Who is with me?"

There were cheers and shouts from around the room. Mena kept her mouth shut. She didn't want anything to do with weapons or fighting. She was relieved to see that Frankie was quiet as well. Even with her knack for mischief, Frankie knew better than to join in on an attack on the castle.

"Excellent," Mark said. "You can sign up at the end of the meeting. We are lucky to have folks so dedicated to our cause."

Thomas raised his hand as if he were taking a lesson.

"Yes, sir? Did you want to sign up?" Mark said.

"Not so fast," Thomas said. "You plan to storm the castle, but what are you going to do when you get there? How do you plan to overthrow the king and queen? Do you think you can just tell them to leave? That's not going to work."

"It's easy. We will kill the king, the queen, the advisors, their staff, anyone sympathetic to them," Mark said. "They are all past reason. The only way to get rid of our oppressors is to eliminate them."

Mena suppressed a whimper. She knew Mark didn't care if people got hurt, but she didn't know he would be so callous about killing. How could someone justify that as easily as he did? She chanced a glance at Frankie. Frankie was staring hard at the table, but Mena could see the fierce girl who had punched Adam.

"Getting into the castle may be a challenge, I will give you that, but we have an advantage," Mark said. "Ladies and gentlemen, I would like you to meet Frances. Frances, please stand up."

Frankie reluctantly rose to her feet. There were gasps all around the room.

"The former princess is going to help us get into the castle," Mark said.

"No, I'm not," Frankie said in a voice that was loud and clear.

Mark laughed. "Oh, don't be shy, sweetheart. Of course, Frances is going to help us, everyone."

"No, I'm not," Frankie said. "I'm not helping you get into the castle. You're a bunch of murderers. You're willing to kill innocent people who get in your way just so you can win. You're as bad as the king and queen. All you care about is getting your way, and you don't care who gets hurt."

"I don't expect you to understand. You're only a child, pretty girl. Come on. Surely, you must not like the king and queen. They kicked you out of that fancy castle, and now you are just one of us. You want to see them dead, don't you?"

Mark had crossed the line. Mena knew what was coming. "Frankie, don't!" she screamed.

Frankie either didn't listen or didn't care. She crashed into Mark and knocked him to the floor. Her fists pounded at his head, his stomach, whatever she could reach.

"Stop! Stop!" Mena yelled, but her shouts weren't doing any good.

David wrapped his arms around Frankie and pulled her away. "Frankie! Let's go!" Angry as she was, Frankie let herself be led away.

"Come on, Mena," Thomas said. He had taken her hand and was leading her toward the door. Mena couldn't remember standing up. How had today gone so wrong? The only answer was Mark. She glanced back at him. His face was bleeding, but he didn't look mad or ashamed. He looked gleeful.

"Good night, Frances!" he called. "You will be a huge help to our revolution."

CHAPTER SIXTEEN

"Do you want me to do that?" Mena offered.

"I can handle it. I'm a doctor, remember? Drink your tea and try to relax," David said.

Frankie sat in silence. She hadn't said a word since the bakery. David had practically carried her out. He had carried her partway here until he decided she could be trusted to walk. Now they were in Thomas' living room. Frankie liked Thomas and David, but she hated this room. She had received too much bad news here. Thomas and Mena were drinking tea. Frankie suspected they had put a bit of alcohol in Mena's to calm her nerves; she had been hysterical.

"How does that feel, Frankie?" David said.

"Cold," Frankie said. He was icing her hands. "Better though." She had been so full of rage. She had forgotten that hitting Mark would also hurt her hands, let alone make a huge scene. Now all of those people would think she was as violent and dangerous as advertised.

Thomas set some candles on the coffee table and lit them.

"What are you doing that for?" David said. "The lamps work perfectly fine."

"The scent is supposed to be calming," Thomas said with a shrug. "That's what the lady at the store said anyway. It's worth a try. We have had quite the evening."

David finally finished examining her hands. "Nothing's broken. You were lucky. Why did you do it? I understand why you hit the guy, but why did you even go to the meeting? Were you thinking of helping them?"

"I went because – " Frankie broke off with a sneeze. Then she sneezed again and again. Maybe she was coming down with a cold. Or maybe it was -. She sneezed some more. She pointed to the candles. "Do you mind?"

"Not at all," Thomas said.

Frankie leaned forward and blew out the candles. Sneezing was annoying, not calming.

"I went because Mark was at our house today while we weren't there. He was snooping around, looking in the windows. I wanted to see what he was up to."

"How do you know he was there if you weren't?" Thomas said.

"Zac told me," Frankie said. She looked up at Thomas. "That's what I wanted to tell you the other day. I figured out my Gift. I'm a Minder, sort of. I can hear animals. If I focus, they can hear my thoughts too."

"Frankie, that's wonderful!" Thomas said. "Not the part about Mark nosing around your house, I don't like the sound of that. Your Gift is incredible. I knew you would figure it out."

Frankie grinned. Strange though her Gift was, he believed her just like that. Even with everything that had happened, he was still on her side.

Thomas took a thoughtful sip of tea. "I think you could benefit from working with a tutor, even if your Gift is unique. Someone proficient in Minding would be best."

"Yes, but it will have to wait. I don't have any money to pay for lessons," Frankie protested.

"I happen to know a Minder who would likely work with you in the evenings after work. He's a friend, so you might even be able to convince him to do the lessons for free," Thomas said.

This sounded too good to be true. "Who?" Frankie said.

"Me," David said.

"You're a Minder? But you're a doctor," Frankie said. She had never given much thought to David's Gift, but he had to be Gifted if he had gone to the meeting as a Gifted ally.

"Not all Minders are security guards and police officers," David said. "I like to help people in a way other than predicting crime. That's why I became a doctor. Minding helps me sometimes. Some patients let me read their thoughts to see exactly what they are feeling, and that helps me figure out how to treat them. Other patients don't like that, and I respect that. My medical training helps me more than anything anyway. I have never trained a Minder – or an Animal Minder – but I would be happy to work with you, Frankie."

"Wow, thank you! Can we start – " Frankie jumped. The candles had relit themselves.

"What's going on? Are they trick candles?" David said.

Trick candles. Frankie knew those. Helen had put them on her birthday cake one year.

"Not that I know of. At least the lady at the store didn't mention it," Thomas said.

"Shall we try blowing them out again?" David suggested.

He and Frankie leaned forward. Then they leapt backward as the flames flared higher. They exchanged a worried glance before the candles extinguished themselves.

"I don't trust that lady at the store," Thomas said. "These candles aren't calming. They're downright dangerous. They're liable to burn the house down turning themselves on and off like that." With that, he gathered the candles and Traveled away. Frankie didn't know where he went. Probably someplace that wasn't too flammable.

** ** **

Zac woke with a start. Something was wrong. He looked for fire. No, there was no fire this time. He could hear someone moving around. He sniffed to see who it was. It was the bad man again. He needed to warn the others. He barked as loud as he could.

Frankie, wake up! he shouted.

Zac, what's going on? Frankie said sleepily.

The bad man is here, Zac said.

Zac ran for the front of the house with Foxy and Frankie right behind him.

"What are you doing?" Mena called groggily.

"Zac said Mark's here," Frankie said.

With that, Mena followed them. Zac wasn't sure what they were going to do. He knew he and Foxy could bite, and Frankie could hit. Then maybe Mena could cook the bad man? For now, Zac ran and barked.

"Call the police," Frankie said.

Zac guessed she was talking to Mena. He didn't know how to call the police.

Foxy shot ahead. She lunged at the bad man. She was very fast, but he was faster. He knocked her to the ground. She let out a whimper.

Zac sunk his teeth into the bad man's leg. He knew dogs weren't supposed to bite people, but this was a bad man who had broken into their house. He held on. The man yelled and hit Zac. It hurt, but Zac didn't let go. There were flashes of light coming from the open door. Zac didn't understand what the lights were, but he held on. The bad man hit him again.

"Leave him alone and get out of our house!" Frankie screamed.

She punched the bad man just like Zac had seen her punch that Adam back at the castle. She punched and shoved, and there were many more flashes of light. Zac could hear Mena crying somewhere, but she sounded far away. Zac wondered how much he and Frankie would have to bite and hit the bad man. A ball of fire flew past them. Zac yelped as the very hot fire brushed by his tail. He wagged his tail to check it out. It hurt but was no longer on fire. The fireball hit the bad man in his unbitten leg. He screamed and lunged for the door. He had had enough of being hurt.

CHAPTER SEVENTEEN

Frankie surveyed the sheep in the field. This was nice work. She got to spend time with the sheep, and most importantly, Mark was not here. Mark was a monster. It was bad enough he had suggested she help kill her own parents, but to top it off, he had broken into their house in the middle of the night. Frankie wanted nothing to do with his plans; she just wanted to be here peacefully with the sheep. Was a peaceful life really too much to ask for?

"Frankie!" Mena shouted.

Frankie turned and saw her sister waving to her from Betty's porch.

"Come inside! Quickly!"

Don't wander off, Frankie told the sheep. She dashed to the house expecting to find some kind of wool emergency. Instead, she found Mena and Betty in front of the television. Since this was Frankie's first job, she didn't know much about breaks. Maybe all jobs had television breaks.

"Mandatory viewing," Betty said simply.

That explained it. People all over the kingdom would be taking breaks for this. Frankie pulled up a chair. The programming started a moment later. Her parents weren't giving today's address. One of their advisors appeared on the screen. He looked very official in a dark suit.

"The kingdom of Superion has been invaded from the north. The military is still investigating, but we suspect we are under attack from Allton. We advise the residents of the northern villages of Superion to be cautious and on alert. We will update when we have more information. Good day."

With that, the mandatory viewing was over, and a soap opera came on. An overly made-up princess was crying about some drama. Frankie didn't watch much television and definitely not these soap operas. Betty didn't seem interested either. She quickly switched off the television.

"Well, that's that," she said.

"An invasion?" Mena said nervously.

"Oh, don't worry about it, dear," Betty said. "We're just minding sheep and spinning wool. There's no need to bother us, right?"

"Right," Frankie said. She looked to Mena.

"Right," Mena said hesitantly.

Frankie knew it was no use telling Mena not to worry. Mena always worried. Frankie stood and was headed for the door when the lights went out. That was followed by a clap of thunder and pouring rain.

Betty sighed. "Summer storm. Frankie, help me get the sheep into the barn. Then we will all eat lunch."

The sheep were frightened by the thunder. Betty called and pulled them into the barn. Frankie did the same thing. She also used her Gift. She hadn't told Betty about her Gift. She liked and trusted Betty, but she also felt it was best if not too many people knew about it yet.

I know the thunder is scary, she said, *but come in the barn. You will be safe there. Come on. It will be alright.*

The Mind speak did seem to calm the sheep. Frankie was grateful for her Gift. The sheep were such peaceful animals; she didn't like to see them frightened.

"You are so good with them," Betty said. "Are you sure you never worked with sheep before?"

Frankie grinned. "I have a way with animals."

Frankie tucked her bare feet up underneath herself and wrapped the blanket tighter. The blanket was a soft wool. Even though she had only been out in the rain for a short time, it had soaked her dress and shoes right through, and now she was freezing. She longed for hot cocoa or a bowl of soup to help her warm up, but all they had was water and cold cheese sandwiches. With no electricity, there weren't many options.

Mena nibbled her sandwich. "Are Allton and Superion enemies?"

Betty took a drink of water. "I told you not to worry about it."

"My sister worries about everything," Frankie said. "We learned about Allton in school, but only a little bit. Allton and Superion are neighbors. They don't bother with each other. They're not enemies, but they're not friends either. We're not going to figure out why they invaded, so there's no use us getting worked up over it."

"Actually, Allton has invaded before, a very long time ago," Betty said.

"Really?" Frankie said. They hadn't learned about that in school, but then again, their history lessons had always been quite limited.

"It was many years ago, generations even. It was long before I was born, and I'm old," Betty said. "People from Allton came, and they said it was to do tests. No one knew what they were testing for or why. The whole thing was very secretive. It was peaceful though. The people from Allton did their supposed tests and went back to their own kingdom. Like I said, it was ages ago, before people even had Gifts. No one knows what happened way back then; maybe it never happened at all."

Frankie made a mental note to ask Thomas about this. He knew a lot about history. Maybe he could tell them more. The invaders from Allton really were none of her business, but Frankie couldn't help being a little curious.

After they finished eating, Betty insisted it was still too wet for Frankie to go outside, so she and Mena taught Frankie how to spin wool. Frankie liked the actual sheep better, but this was nice work too. She liked to watch the fluffy wool turn to yarn. Betty and Mena were able to knit beautiful things out of the yarn, but not Frankie. Knitting was one of those skills like cooking; princesses simply didn't learn. Frankie guessed Mena could teach her how to knit someday, but for today she was content to spin wool and wait for the rain to end. The time passed slowly. After what seemed like forever, the sun came out, and the power came back on.

"Ah, that's better," Betty said.

"I'll go back out with the sheep," Frankie said.

She abandoned the wool and ran outside. She ran to the barn and threw open the door.

The storm is over. Come on out, Frankie called.

The sheep ambled out of the barn and looked around cautiously. *No more scary thunder,* many of them said.

No more scary thunder, just sunshine, Frankie confirmed.

The sheep returned to their grazing. As they grazed, Frankie wondered if they knew what their wool was used for, so she told them. She showed them how she had learned to spin wool. She showed them the pretty blankets and clothes Betty and Mena could make from the wool. The older sheep knew all about wool, but this was news to some of the younger sheep.

Cool! a cute little sheep said. *I thought I was just getting a haircut! I like when Betty cuts my hair because if she doesn't, it gets too hot.*

I see someone! one of the brave sheep at the edge of the field said.

Frankie walked toward him. *Who is it? It's not the man from yesterday, is it?*

No, it's not him. It's two people. They just got out of a car. There are a lot of cars.

Scary cars, another sheep said. *Loud, smelly cars.*

No, don't worry about the cars, Frankie said. *They're not going to hurt us.* Frankie stood at the fence and watched the two people walking down the road. It looked like a man and a woman, although from the distance, Frankie couldn't tell much more than that.

"Hello," the woman called when she spotted Frankie.

"Hello," Frankie replied. She tried to sound friendly, but she was a little nervous. She gripped the staff in her hand tighter than was really necessary. Usually she was flanked by her parents or Mena; she wasn't used to meeting strangers on her own. She willed herself to be calm. These people were just walking as far as she knew. Then they stopped in front of her.

"Can I help you? Are you looking for Betty?" Frankie offered as she regarded the strangers. They were tall and dressed almost identically in dark shirts and dark pants. Frankie was used to women and girls wearing dresses, although maybe women in slacks was common in the country. She was so used to city fashion and wearing what she was told. The woman's sandy brown hair was pulled back off her face. There was nothing glamorous or flashy about these two, but they didn't look like they belonged here in the country. They seemed too refined somehow.

"No, we're not here for Betty. We actually came here to speak with you, Frances," the woman said.

Without meaning to, Frankie took a step backward. The sheep sensed her fear. *More bad people! Use the staff!* they said.

"We don't mean to scare you," the man said quickly. "We come here in peace. My name is King Sean, and this is my wife, Queen Izabel."

"King and Queen of what?" Frankie said warily. Had someone overthrown her parents already?

"Allton," King Sean said.

"The television!" Frankie said. "You're the invaders."

"Yes, we're the invaders they're so concerned about, but I promise we don't mean you any harm, Frances," King Sean said. "We're looking to remove your parents from power, and you and your Gift can help us do that."

"Why does everyone think I want to kill my parents?" Frankie wailed. "No, I won't help you." She resisted the urge to lash out and punch him. Instead, she turned and ran for the house, leaving this new king and queen and the sheep behind her.

"Frankie! Please come back!" Queen Izabel called.

Frankie stopped in her tracks. "What did you call me?"

"Frankie. You like that better than Frances, don't you?" Queen Izabel said.

Yes, she told practically everyone to call her Frankie, but she had just met Queen Izabel and King Sean, and the topic of name preferences hadn't come up. "How do you know that?"

"We've been keeping an eye on you and the rest of Superion for a long time," Queen Izabel said. "Please don't be afraid. We're a peaceful people. We don't want to see your parents killed. We don't want to see anyone killed for that matter. This rebellion is deeply troubling to us. As much as we don't want to interfere, we think it best to remove your parents from their current positions, without harming them of course. As my husband mentioned, you can help us do that."

"How?" Frankie said. This sounded too good to be true. Could these people she had just met really be on her side?

"First, you need to get to the castle," King Sean said.

Frankie's eyes flicked to the cars at the end of the street. "Are you taking me?"

"No, we're going to meet you there," King Sean said. "You should go with Mark and the rebels. Make them think you're with them. Then break off and sneak the king and queen out of the castle. I have to admit that the people of Allton don't understand the specifics of the Gifts as you do. You will have to come up with an exact plan on your own, and we don't expect you to go alone. Bring your Gifted friends to help you."

"My Gifted friends?" Frankie repeated. How much did these people know about her?

"And your sister," Queen Izabel added. "I'm sure her Gift can help you as well."

"How do you know about my sister? How do you know about her Gift?" Frankie realized all she was doing was asking questions. She probably wasn't coming across as knowledgeable or intelligent.

"We don't know much about Filomena, but with such a powerful family, she certainly must have a powerful Gift," King Sean said. "We must be on our way, but we will see you by the castle tomorrow. Good luck."

As King Sean and Queen Izabel bid her goodbye and good luck, Frankie could only wave. She was still just a child, and not even a royal child anymore. Even with help, how was she supposed to pull this off? What had she gotten into?

"Frankie!" Betty called, pulling her away from her wonderings. She saw she was being waved to the house. She offered the sheep some comforting thoughts as she jogged.

"Yes?"

"More mandatory viewing. You better come in. Who was that you were talking to anyway?"

"No one. They were lost and needed directions," Frankie fibbed as she took a seat next to Mena.

The same advisor from earlier appeared on the screen. Before he could get a word out, he was replaced by someone in a dark mask.

"This is the signal. It is time to unite and attack. Our allies are many, and we will be victorious." The voice of the masked man was familiar, and Frankie had a good idea who it was.

The scene switched. Frankie recognized herself in her pajamas with her short hair messy. She was kicking and punching someone whose face was blurred out. They wanted people to think that Frankie was one of the rebels, but of course, they didn't want anyone to know the person she was fighting was one of the rebel leaders. Frankie saw the dogs jumping and biting, and she saw a fireball fly over their heads. She had been so overwhelmed the night before that she hadn't thought much of the fire. She had assumed it was Mark's doing, but now she didn't think so.

Thomas, David, and Mena stared at her. Frankie looked down at her tea self-consciously. She was getting tired of tea. Didn't they ever drink anything else in Aurora? She had just told everyone about her meeting with King Sean and Queen Izabel. They were her only friends; they were the only people she had to tell.

"We know next to nothing about Allton. Can we trust these people?" David said.

Frankie looked up but didn't say anything. King Sean and Queen Izabel had seemed nice enough, but David was right. Just how trustworthy were they?

Thomas looked thoughtful. "Well, I for one don't want to sit idly by. We need to pick a side. Can we trust the rebels?"

"Absolutely not," Mena said. She twisted her hands in her lap nervously. "All the rebels want to do is use Frankie to hurt people. They even broke into our house to get a video of her. Who knows what they may do to her next. At least these Allton royals claim to be peaceful."

Frankie took a deep breath. "I think I have to take my chances, go to the castle and hope to meet up with the Allton royals," she said. "I doubt Mark would let me stay home and mind my own business. He would probably drag me along by force. You all don't have to come with me if you don't want to; I can figure out a plan on my own." Frankie didn't quite believe herself on the last part. She didn't want to put her friends in danger, but she knew she could use their help.

"I will come with you," Thomas said. "If we have Gifts, we might as well use them. Maybe you could use a Traveler on your side."

"You might need a Minder. I'll come too," David said.

Mena sighed. "I will go because I might as well worry there than worry here, but I don't know what help I'll be. I don't have a Gift."

Frankie was relieved to have their support, and she had news for Mena. "Actually, I think I figured out what your Gift is. You can start fires."

Mena laughed. "Of course, I can start fires with matches. I've been doing it my whole life. Anyone can."

"No, I don't mean it like that," Frankie said. "You just do. I've seen you."

"Now you're being ridiculous. I don't have a Gift," Mena said, shaking her head. "I have accepted that, and you need to too. Let's stop wasting time. We need to plan."

"I have seen you start fires," Frankie persisted. "You did it at the bakery, and you did it again last night to scare Mark away."

"You did it here too," David said. "Remember the trick candles?"

Mena didn't protest. She looked too flustered to speak.

"It makes a lot of sense," Thomas said. "A Fire Gift sure is unheard of, but so is Frankie's Gift. We can plan on the bus. In the meantime, let's practice the Gifts. Frankie, you're with David. Mena, you're with me."

** ** **

Mena followed Thomas into the backyard. She had her doubts about this. She imagined this must have been what Frankie had felt like going into her unsuccessful Gift lessons. They all liked Frankie's silly idea that she had some kind of Fire Gift. It was nonsense. Surely, Mark or someone had set the fires to scare them. Thomas brought an armful of candles and a bucket of water into the yard. The water was a nice precaution, but it was unnecessary. There wouldn't be any fires unless someone found some matches.

"Doggies, please stay by the house like Frankie told you. Good doggies," Thomas said.

Mena glanced at Zac and Foxy. She would prefer not to have an audience for her lesson, but at least she knew the dogs wouldn't judge her when she remained Not Gifted.

Thomas set the candles on the ground and stood back a safe distance. "I have never seen anyone with a Fire Gift before, let alone taught one. I suppose it's a bit like Reaching, like you are reaching for the fire. In any case, we teach all of the Gifts the same way. Please try to be as calm as possible and focus."

Mena was such a worrier; calm was going to be a challenge. "I don't think I started the other fires, but even if I did, I wasn't calm then. I was worried, and last night I was just plain scared." As she said this, half of the candles burst into flame.

"I know this is quite a shock, but who else could have done that just now?" Thomas said.

Mena shrugged. She knew it wasn't Thomas; he wouldn't trick her like that. It couldn't be one of the dogs; animals weren't Gifted in the way that people were. That left Mena. After years of believing she was Not Gifted, could she really have a never before seen Gift? It was like finding out she was an entirely different person.

"I think I did that," she finally said in a shaky whisper as she watched the flames dance.

"This is a powerful Gift," Thomas said. "You will have to be careful with it. Were you focusing when you lit the candles just now?"

Mena shook her head. "No, I was too worried. I'm always worried."

"Ah. Intent is the recommended way to use a Gift, but emotion can trigger it too. It's quite common for children. I know from experience. I had nightmares as a child. Imagine how much scarier it was when in addition to having a nightmare, I woke up in a strange place. Turns out I was Traveling in my sleep."

"And you don't have problems with that anymore?"

"No, I haven't had problems with that in years. My teachers taught me to be calm and focus, and that's what I'm going to teach you now."

Mena knew he was right. She couldn't let her emotions get the best of her. Her worries had almost burnt down the bakery.

"I don't know if I can," she admitted as a few more candles lit up.

"I think you can. You've shone under pressure before. You worked in the castle, and that must have been a stressful job."

"Yes, I guess," Mena said. "I've always been a worrier, but things have never been like this. The rebels have my nerves on edge."

"Unfortunately, rebels and revolutions are part of our lives now," Thomas said kindly. "Until our lives go back to peace and quiet, breathe and focus."

** ** **

Frankie sat in the passenger seat of David's car. Sitting up front was new and strangely exciting. Everyone had always insisted she sit in the back.

"Can you still hear them?" David said.

Zac? Frankie said.

Hi Frankie!

Frankie! Foxy said, not wanting to be left out.

"Yes," Frankie said. They were testing the limits of her Gift. How far would they have to go before she couldn't hear the dogs anymore?

You should see Mena lighting all these candles! Zac said.

"Do you like your Gift?" David said. "It is rather unique, and it's not like we get to choose our Gifts."

"Oh, yes!" Frankie said. "I have always loved animals, and if I'm the only person to ever have this Gift, I am very lucky. Do you like being a Minder?"

"Yes, I do. I'm able to use it in my work to help people, but I have to admit I have heard a lot of thoughts I wish I didn't."

Frankie could believe that. People must have much more revealing thoughts than animals.

"How about now?" David said. "Can you still hear them?"

Frankie tried and got another enthusiastic response from Zac and Foxy.

"Incredible," David said. He looked impressed.

"Why? How far are we anyway?"

"A mile. A Minder having this kind of reach is unheard of."

"How far is your reach?"

"If I'm really lucky, I can hear someone in the next room. Most Minders have to be in the same room as the person they're trying to hear."

Frankie, can you hear me? Frankie, there's someone here, Zac said.

He's doing scary things, Foxy said.

CHAPTER EIGHTEEN

Frankie wished David would drive faster. She tapped her feet nervously. She wanted to know what was going on! Even though they were close enough that she could hear the dogs again, Zac and Foxy would only say "strange boy" and "scary things." Whoever this boy was, Frankie hoped Mena managed to scare him off with the fire before he hurt any of them. When they finally got to the house, Frankie jumped out of the car and sprinted to the backyard with David close behind her. David may be bigger and stronger, but she was faster.

Frankie saw a boy about her own age with dark curly hair that flopped into his eyes. This must be the strange boy. There wasn't any fire in sight. What was Mena waiting for?

"Stop!" Frankie screamed. She didn't know what this boy was up to, but if the dogs said he was scary, he must be up to no good.

"It's okay. It's just Henry," David said as he came up behind her.

"Frankie, I would like you to meet Henry. He's my student," Thomas said. He was as calm as ever.

Frankie was confused. Thomas and David knew this boy? What were they doing associating with someone scary? Also, why were they looking at her like she was crazy?

"The dogs were frightened," Frankie said. She realized she sounded defensive. Zac and Foxy hid behind her, and they peeked out at Henry warily. Frankie bent to pet and comfort them. Henry stared at her with an undisguised look of dislike.

"I recognize this girl. She's the princess you left me to teach, and she turned out to be useless," Henry spat. "Everyone knows it. All the brat does is go around and hit people. The rebels must really be hopeless to enlist this one."

Frankie didn't notice herself step forward, but she felt David restrain her. How could Thomas and David let him talk like that? She glanced toward Mena. The candles at her feet burned, but she seemed calmer than normal, not her usual flustered self.

Thomas sighed. "You will have to excuse Henry, Frankie. Charm is not his specialty. He came here tonight because he is thinking of joining the rebels and wanted my advice. I think he should join our group, our secret group. He is quite talented."

Henry folded his arms across his chest. "The only reason I would go with you and whatever your secret is is because of Thomas. I don't care about some former princess. We're probably better off without her anyway."

Zac and Foxy sent Frankie pictures of the scary things, and suddenly they made sense. "You're a Reacher," she stated. "Thomas is right. You're not charming, but we could use a Reacher. It's the one Gift we lack, and it's bound to come in handy."

"How did you know that?" Henry asked. His attitude shifted. He didn't seem arrogant now, more like fearful. "Did you just read my mind? Because that would be really rude if you did. Are you some kind of secret Minder the king and queen don't know about?"

"Something like that. I'm not as useless as you think," Frankie said.

** ** **

Zac trotted along proudly at Frankie's side. Frankie was wearing pants like a boy. That was new. Frankie always wore dresses. This felt adventurous, going off in the dark as they were. They would be taking something called a bus to the castle. Zac wondered if they were going back to the castle to stay. He had wanted to bring his teddy bear, but Mena said they had to pack light. Zac nudged Foxy. He was glad she was coming with them. She was a good buddy.

There was a giant car up ahead. Was that what was taking them to the castle? It was huge! He asked Frankie about it.

"Yes, that's our bus," Frankie said.

"Who are you talking to?" the Reacher boy, Henry, asked.

Frankie didn't answer him. Zac didn't blame her. He had been scary. Then Zac saw an even scarier person. The man who had broken into their house stood at the door of the bus. Was he going to the castle too? Why hadn't Mena cooked him when she had the chance?

"Where do you think you're going?" the man, Mark, asked.

"We're going with you. You do want our help, don't you?" Thomas said.

"Some of you, yes. Not you." Mark pointed at Frankie.

Zac growled at him. No one should be mean to Frankie.

"That's hypocritical," Thomas said. "You broke into her house to take video of her that you would later use to support your cause. Including her in your trip to the castle is the least you could do."

"Fine," Mark said. "The girl can come, but not those mutts."

Zac growled again. He didn't like this man, and he didn't like being called a mutt.

"We need them," Frankie said. "They can help."

"How can they help?" Mark said. "They're stupid animals. Besides, the bus will be crowded enough as it is."

Then Mena did something wonderful. She lit Mark on fire, just the hem of his pant leg. He was so silly that he didn't notice it right away. Zac and Foxy barked to get his attention. As much as they didn't like him, someone should tell him he was on fire. He looked down, and when he saw the fire, he screamed. Then he dropped to the ground and rolled. That put the fire out. He looked very silly; people weren't supposed to roll like that.

"See, the dogs helped you just now," Thomas said. "They saved you from what would have been some nasty burns."

"Fine," Mark grumbled as he stood up. "The dogs can come, but make sure they don't take up too much room."

Lots of people looked at Zac and Foxy as they walked down the aisle of the bus; they were probably the only dogs here. Zac shared a bench with Frankie and Foxy. He sat on Frankie's lap, and Foxy cuddled up next to them. After a minute, the bus started to move. Zac tried to look out the window to watch the scenery, but it was too dark to see anything. He also felt a little nauseous. As exciting as the bus had looked, maybe it would make him sick like the car had. It would probably be best to take a nap. It was nighttime, and he was tired anyway.

** ** **

Mena was burning up in her heavy outfit on the warm bus. She shrugged out of her jacket. It was really David's jacket. They had disguised Frankie as best they could. If they were going into Superion City and the castle, they at least had to try to blend in. Frankie had insisted Mena be disguised as well. Mena didn't really think that was necessary, but she had played along. She wore some of David's old clothes. It felt strange to wear pants instead of a dress.

Mena shared a seat with Henry. She had thought Frankie was a handful, but despite her knack for trouble, Frankie really was a sweet girl. Henry, on the other hand, was all attitude. He seemed to have respect for Thomas, but that was about it. If she had to sit next to the boy for a few hours, maybe she should try to make conversation.

"So you're a Reacher," she said.

Henry rolled his eyes. "Obviously. You saw me practicing. What's your Gift?"

"Mine is a little unusual, just like Frankie's," Mena said.

"You girls think you're so special with your unusual Gifts," Henry said. "I bet it's all an act. I think you're making it all up. You probably don't even have Gifts."

The boy was definitely a brat, but something about his bravado

162

seemed off. "There's nothing wrong with being Not Gifted," Mena said.

"I never said I didn't like the Not Gifted," Henry said defensively. "Not all of them are bad. My parents are Not Gifted."

That was odd. "Your parents are Not Gifted, and you are?"

"Sometimes Gifts skip generations. It's rare, but it happens, okay?" Henry said. He looked like he had said more than he meant to.

Mena nodded. "I've heard of that."

"Don't tell anyone, would you?" he said. "It's supposed to be a secret. Ever since I got my Test results last year, people keep trying to put me in a home for Gifted kids, but I don't want to go. I want to stay with my family. They're all I have."

"Your secret's safe with me," she said.

"Thanks," he said, but he still looked uneasy.

Mena wasn't sure if she should do it, but why not? People were bound to find out eventually. "I know how important family is," she said. "Frankie is my sister. I would do anything to protect her."

Henry looked at her curiously, like he wasn't sure whether to believe her. "If you're sisters, how come she was a princess and you were not?"

Mena shrugged. "Sometimes that's how things work out. I'm going to try to get some sleep. We have a long day tomorrow. Good night."

"Good night."

** ** **

Frankie slept fitfully. The bus was warm, and the two dogs asleep against her made her even warmer. Her dreams were full of fire. She didn't know if that was brought on by the warmth or by the revelation of Mena's Gift.

Oh no, I know this place! Zac thought.

Frankie opened her eyes. It was just getting light outside. She knew this place too. It was where she rescued him. She hugged him. She saved him that day, and she intended to keep him safe. The bus slowed. Was everyone going on foot from here? That would make more sense than driving right up to the castle.

Mark stood up at the front. "Everyone listen up!" he shouted.

Frankie saw several people jump. Half of the bus had been asleep.

"We will break off into small groups so that we can get through the city unnoticed. There is a morning address planned. That is when we will make our attack. We will attack from the north, and the other rebel groups will attack from the other sides. Remember, the key is to overwhelm the king and queen. Kill them if you can, but don't forget they are Travelers. There is very little to keep them from Traveling away. That is why we must overwhelm their senses. There are many of us and only two of them. We can do this. Victory and equality will be ours. Are there any questions?"

The bus was quiet except for excited murmurings. Frankie didn't like the instruction of "kill them if you can," but she knew better than to speak up. She kept her mouth shut.

"Well then, I will start to dismiss you. Stay in your seats until I tell you," Mark instructed. He let people off the bus in twos and threes. He started in the front. Frankie knew she and her friends still had a wait; they were three-quarters of the way back.

Frankie, I have to go potty, Foxy said.

We'll be outside soon, Frankie said. *We have to wait our turn.*

But I have to go now! Foxy said. She whimpered. *I don't want to have an accident. That would be so embarrassing!*

Frankie tried to shush and soothe Foxy, but it was no use. She really had to go.

"Shut that dog up!" someone said rudely.

"Sorry. She has to go out," Frankie said.

"Never should have let dogs on a bus in the first place. Mark, let them out before they stink up the whole bus," the rude person said.

Frankie usually didn't like rude people, but this time she was grateful. She and her friends were off the bus a minute later. Foxy and Zac relieved themselves immediately.

I feel better now, Foxy said.

Me too, Zac said.

Frankie looked around. The winding city streets were so familiar. "We're here and off the bus. Now what?"

"Did the king and queen say where to meet them?" Thomas said.

"Wait!" Henry said. "We're meeting the king and queen? That's your secret plan? That doesn't make sense at all."

Frankie didn't feel like explaining herself to Henry. "Not the king and queen you're thinking of. No, they didn't say. They just said to take the bus here."

"Then they must be close," Thomas said. "They might even be watching us right now. Let's walk. I'm sure we'll meet up with them soon."

Frankie didn't argue with this plan. It was the only one they had, and it made sense. She held Zac's leash. Foxy wanted to walk with Mena. Frankie had adventured through these city streets many times. The purpose of her previous adventures had been to have a little fun; the stakes of this adventure were much higher.

Zac stopped next to a dark car. *I think someone's in there*, he said. *And I smell blood.*

Frankie reported this to the group.

Henry huffed. "Dogs can't talk. You're being ridiculous."

"Dogs can too talk. Just not many people can hear them," Frankie said. She nodded toward the car. "Come on. It might be them. This looks an awful lot like the car I saw yesterday." She tried to look in the windows, but it was no good. It was the fancy dark glass like Superion's royal cars had; it was impossible to see inside.

"We have Gifts. We knew we would have to use them today," David said. He closed his eyes, and Frankie recognized his look of focused concentration.

He opened his eyes a moment later. "There are three people inside, two men and a woman. They have been beaten and are hurt badly."

"We have to help them, even if it's not King Sean and Queen Izabel," Frankie said. She knocked on the door and hoped for an answer.

"Allow me," Henry said. Using his Gift of Reach, he unlocked the door and opened it.

Frankie gasped when she saw the scene inside the car. There was blood everywhere. King Sean and the other man were unconscious; the other man must be the driver. Queen Izabel was awake, but she was in bad shape. She lay crumpled on the seat. Her face was covered in bruises, and her eyes were almost swollen shut. Nevertheless, her eyes lit up when she saw Frankie.

"There you are, Frankie," Queen Izabel said in a raspy voice. "I knew you would come." She coughed. "I heard you out there, and I tried to open the door, but I think my arm is broken. What of the rebels? When do they plan to attack?"

"The morning address," Frankie said.

"Then you need to be quick and get your parents out of there before that," Queen Izabel whispered. "I'm afraid we cannot go with you. Not like this. We would only slow you down. Bring the king and queen here with a television camera. Hopefully, we can have them announce their resignation in front of all of Superion without any more violence. Be brave, Frankie. I know you can do this task."

Frankie shook her head. "We can't leave you like this. Who did this to you anyway?"

"Superion soldiers. We were lucky. We got away, but barely. That was probably what today's morning address was supposed to be about, how the invaders had been captured. Now it will be that we're still on the loose and dangerous. I'm sure we look capable of doing dangerous things right now, don't we? But yes, you do have to leave us. Go on. You're wasting time."

Frankie was torn. They didn't have much time, but no matter what Queen Izabel said, she didn't feel comfortable leaving them. What if the soldiers found them? They weren't in any condition to defend themselves.

"I will stay with them," David said.

Frankie sighed with relief. David to the rescue.

"You're the Minder, aren't you?" Queen Izabel said. "Go help Frankie. She needs you. Leave us."

"I may be a Minder, but as a doctor, I cannot in good conscience leave you like this," David said. "They have enough Gifts to aid them. I'm staying with you." He didn't sound like he could be convinced any other way.

Foxy nudged Frankie's hand. *Frankie, can I stay too? I try to be brave, but breaking into the castle sounds awfully scary. Would it be too much trouble if I stayed with David?*

Frankie rubbed Foxy's head. She voiced Foxy's request.

David had climbed into the car and started to examine his patients. He gave Frankie and Foxy a distracted nod.

"She can be our guard dog," Queen Izabel said with an attempt at a smile. With all of her bruises, it looked painful.

CHAPTER NINETEEN

Mena had considered coming back to the city someday, but she hadn't expected it to be like this. She adjusted the hat that was part of her disguise. She wasn't used to wearing hats, but if they passed any of her few acquaintances in the city, she would go unrecognized. Mena glanced at Frankie. With her short hair and wearing a very old pair of trousers that she had borrowed from David, she looked boyish, but she wasn't going to pass for a boy. She was too pretty for that. Thomas and Henry were also wearing hats, but considering they didn't know many people in the city, it was unlikely anyone would notice them. Mena put her hands in her pockets. It felt strange to be empty-handed. She missed holding on to Foxy, but she didn't blame the dog for wanting to stay behind.

"Who were those people back there? Were they some kind of made-up king and queen?" Henry said.

"King Sean and Queen Izabel. They're the king and queen of Allton," Thomas said.

Mena kept her eyes down as they walked. The winding streets were starting to fill with people. It was that time of the morning when people were hustling off to work or to the shops.

"How do you know they're really the king and queen?" Henry said. "How do you know they're really trying to help us? You're not taking her word for it, are you?" He pointed at Frankie. The attitude was back. The compassionate boy Mena had briefly met on the bus was gone.

"Why would I lie?" Frankie said hotly.

"King Sean and Queen Izabel have been through a lot," Thomas said. "Do you really think they would go to all this trouble if they didn't care about us? Besides, David just read their minds. Would he stay behind to help them if they were our enemy?"

Henry sighed. "I guess not, but what about our king and queen? How are we supposed to get them out of the castle? What's your plan?"

Mena had to admit she was wondering the same thing. Thomas was intelligent and must have a good plan, but she was still worried.

"Actually, you just saw our plan," Thomas said. "The trick with David using his Gift to see if anyone was there, then you using your Gift to unlock the door for us."

"Right, well, we just lost our Minder, so that plan is out," Henry said. "Time to come up with a Plan B, although the idea of getting the king and queen to come with us is absurd. If I had known that was what your plan was about, I would have just joined the rebels."

"Why don't you then?" Frankie snapped. "No one's keeping you here."

"Maybe because I don't want to associate with a group of people who are so eager to be murderers," Henry said. "I don't like you, but you're better than the alternative."

Frankie made a face.

"Children, please stop fighting," Thomas said patiently. "Given that we no longer have David's help, I will get us into the castle. I will Travel in. Then I will let the rest of you in."

Mena couldn't help but protest. "That sounds too risky. What if you Travel right into the arms of a guard while we're all outside waiting for you?"

"Yes, it is risky, but don't worry, Mena, we will get in," Thomas said.

Didn't Thomas know her by now? She was a worrier. She worried about little everyday things, so of course, she was going to worry about an extremely dangerous thing like sneaking into the castle. Even though it was dangerous and scary, she knew they had to follow through with this. She just wished there was a safer way to sneak a group of people into the castle. Frankie had snuck Zac in using a bag the day she had rescued him. That had worked for him. He was only a puppy. Such a strategy would not work for people unless they found someone willing to sneak them in using body bags, and that thought was just morbid.

The wind blew, knocking the hat from her head. She reached to fix it over her fair hair.

"Mena? Is that you?" someone called.

She froze.

"I didn't know you were still in the city, but I guess you have to find work after what happened with the princess, you poor dear."

Mena located the speaker. Her arms were so full of packages that the bundle practically stretched over her head. Mena could barely see her face, but she would recognize her old friend anywhere.

"Helen! It is so nice to see you," Mena said, and it really was a pleasant surprise. "What are you doing with all that? Are big shopping trips part of your retirement?"

"Retirement, ha! That plan didn't quite work out," Helen said as she adjusted her pile of shopping bags. "This is all for Joey."

"Who's Joey?"

"The heir."

That threw Mena for a loop. How did the king and queen have an heir lined up? Did she and Frankie have a brother they didn't know about?

"I have an idea," Frankie piped up. "We'll help you carry those packages. It will get us into the castle."

Helen's eyes drifted over the rest of Mena's party. She stared at Frankie in shock. Even with a new haircut and a disguise, Helen would recognize Frankie anywhere.

"No, I won't let you into the castle," Helen said. She stood up as tall as her heavy packages would let her. "I saw you on television. You're helping the rebels. I saw you hurt that poor man, and now you want to hurt your own mother and father. I always knew you liked mischief, but I never knew you were just plain mean."

Frankie stomped her foot impatiently. "We are not helping the rebels, and that was not a poor man. That jerk broke into our house in the middle of the night. We were defending ourselves."

"Come on, Helen," Mena pleaded. "You raised Frankie. You know her better than anyone. Do you really think she would join a group that wants to kill her parents? Is she evil?"

Helen sighed. "I guess not," she said reluctantly. "But why do you have to get into the castle?"

"We need to rescue my parents," Frankie said. "We need to get them out of there before anyone hurts them."

Helen looked like she would rather be anywhere else. "Fine, I'll bring you in, but that's it," she said. "If anyone asks, I'll say you work in one of the shops and offered to help me. I don't want any part of your adventure though. I'm too old for that sort of thing."

"Thank you," Mena said. She was so grateful that she could hug Helen, but instead, she relieved her of some of her packages.

Helen stared at Zac. "What about that dog? You know animals aren't allowed in the castle. Can't you leave him somewhere?"

"He's part of the team. He comes with us," Frankie said.

Helen looked to mutter a prayer but didn't argue.

** ** **

Frankie, I'm hungry, Zac said.

Frankie didn't blame him. They hadn't had anything to eat since dinner the night before, and that felt like ages ago now. It didn't help that they were currently surrounded by food. Helen had stashed them in the pantry. Frankie wished Helen hadn't been so quick to get rid of them, but she didn't blame her. Just getting them into the castle had been a lot to ask, and it was a huge help. Without Helen, they would probably be hiding outside right now.

"Me too," Frankie said. "We might as well eat while we plan our next move."

"I doubt you were talking to me, but I'm starving," Henry said.

They made themselves cold sandwiches. Zac happily ate one. Frankie would have preferred oatmeal. It must still be breakfast time, but cooking in the kitchen probably wasn't a good idea. It was one thing to hide in the pantry, but if the cook saw strangers cooking in her kitchen, she would probably have a heart attack.

"We're in, now what?" Frankie asked Thomas. He was older and wiser than the rest of them. Surely, he knew what they should do next.

Thomas almost looked sheepish. "Well, you could talk to them. You're their daughter. They love you. They will listen to you."

Frankie shook her head. She didn't like that plan. She had been expecting it; it was obvious. Still, she didn't have much faith that it would work.

"They don't love me. They disowned me because they thought I was Not Gifted. What kind of parents do that? They won't listen to me."

"Maybe not, but we have to try," Thomas said.

Henry swallowed the last bite of his second sandwich. "If it doesn't work, I can throw things at them until we scare them into coming with us," he said.

Frankie almost smiled. That was maybe the only intelligent thing she had heard Henry say.

Mena looked like she was having second thoughts about this whole ordeal. She had only managed to eat half of her sandwich. Frankie watched as Mena fed her other half sandwich to Zac. Zac, always grateful for food, wagged his tail as he ate. Frankie knew Mena. She was probably too nervous to eat.

Frankie sighed. Thomas was right. She had to at least try the talk it over approach. She squared her shoulders.

"I'm not going up there alone. I want all of you to come with me."

No one argued. Frankie led the way through the castle's corridors. She gripped Zac's leash tightly. She shivered. It was always so cold in the castle. She had forgotten that. David's old clothes were warmer than a dress, but it was still cold. The colorful tapestries and paintings on the walls were a blur as she walked. Her parents would be in their private quarters, a place Frankie had rarely visited in her whole time living in the castle and now she was breaking in. She stopped in her tracks when she saw the guard stationed at the door.

Keep going. We can take him, Zac said. He pulled at his leash.

Frankie wished she could borrow some of Zac's optimism; she really had her doubts about this. She hoped the panic wasn't showing on her face. "I'm here to see my parents," she announced. At least her voice came out braver than she felt.

Zac gave a bark of agreement.

"Of course, Princess," the guard said with a smile. He stepped aside.

This was too easy. Frankie wasn't a princess anymore. She was an intruder. The guards should be protecting her parents from her. Something didn't feel right. Then a vase of flowers careened into the guard's head. He crumpled to the floor. Henry. Mena let out a small scream.

Is he dead? Zac said.

Frankie repeated the question out loud as she stared at the unmoving guard.

"No, just knocked out," Henry said.

"Thank you for defending us, but was that really necessary? He could have brain damage or something," Frankie said.

"He wasn't that smart to begin with," Henry said. "He's just fast. That's why he's here already. He's not one of the royal guards. He's one of the rebels. He was in my class at primary school. What are you waiting for? Get in there before he wakes up."

Frankie reached for the unguarded door, but before she could open it, it swung toward them.

"What is all of the commotion out here?" Queen Veronica demanded. She wore a fine purple dress, and her hair and makeup were perfect. Clearly, she was ready for the camera and the morning address.

"Oh, it's just the rebels," the queen said dryly. She looked amused as she gazed at them. "Here to kill us, sweetheart? I don't think you have it in you. All of the useless Not Gifted running around trying to look tough and important. It's all so silly."

Zac barked. He was tough.

"Back with that mutt of yours, are you?" King Leopold roared as he came to join the queen.

"We're here to help you," Frankie said. "We need to protect you from the rebels. They're already here in the castle. We have to leave quickly." She couldn't help shivering as she spoke. She knew shivering wouldn't help her look brave or tough, but it was cold.

The king laughed. "Look at her. She's desperate. I knew turning her out completely was a bad idea. We should have given her some money so she wouldn't have reason to come back here with some nonsense story. It's pathetic. Look at how she's shaking. She's just a useless, Not Gifted brat like all the rest. Guard!"

Frankie stuck to Thomas' plan even though it was clearly not working. "Please. It's not nonsense. We're trying to help. Come with us."

The king shook his head. "Not Gifted brat."

Now Frankie started to get mad. "That's not true! I am Gifted. I'm an Animal Minder." Why couldn't they believe that she was here to help? Why couldn't Henry throw another vase or something? Maybe that would knock some sense into them.

"Oh dear, she really is making up stories now, isn't she?" Queen Veronica said. "Guard!"

Thomas tried to intervene. "Please, your Majesties, everything Frankie is saying is true – "

"Oh, you're here, are you?" King Leopold cut in. He seemed to notice the rest of the group for the first time. "You were supposed to be a first class tutor, but I guess that's not true if you're associating with this lot."

Stop being mean to my friends! Zac said. He barked and barked.

"I'll get rid of that annoying mutt once and for all," King Leopold said. He charged forward. Frankie tried to stop him, but he was too quick. He grabbed Zac, and Zac yelped.

"Let him go! You're hurting him!" Frankie shrieked.

Frankie, help me! Zac cried.

Frankie, we're in trouble. They're going to hurt us! Foxy said from the car.

It was all too much. Being able to hear the dogs was an amazing Gift, but now it wasn't enough. There was trouble everywhere, and Frankie didn't know how to fix it. All she could do was listen and feel hopeless. There was nothing else for it; she channeled the angry girl who had attacked Adam and Mark. She ignored the fact that her father was nearly twice her size and flung herself at him, but she was too late. He was gone. He had already Traveled away with Zac in hand.

Frankie! Zac screamed.

She could still hear him. That meant he was close. She couldn't let him down. She had to save him.

CHAPTER TWENTY

Mena stood between Thomas and Henry. The three of them were locked in a staring match with Queen Veronica. Mena probably should have run after Frankie, but she had been too shocked to move. It was like she was frozen in the queen's stare.

"What are you all still doing here? Run along," Queen Veronica said. She sounded bored.

"Please come with us. We want to help you," Mena said in a small voice. The talk it out approach hadn't worked for Frankie. Mena doubted it would work for her, but she had to at least try.

Queen Veronica laughed. "How can a useless Not Gifted servant girl help me? You're nothing but trouble. I never would have hired you if Helen hadn't recommended you. I shouldn't have listened to her." She turned to return to her quarters and the television camera.

Mena felt tears sting her eyes. She knew Queen Veronica was often cruel, but her words hurt more than Mena had expected. "But I'm your daughter," she whispered.

The queen turned back at Mena's whisper and stared at her in shock. Clearly, Helen hadn't explained her reason for the recommendation. "If that's true, we were right to give you up. Useless –"

"I've had enough of this," Henry muttered.

A heavy book soared toward Queen Veronica's head. It almost hit her. She Traveled to the other side of the room to avoid it. Henry didn't relent. He threw books, chairs, everything he could find. The queen kept Traveling. She took knocks from some of the chairs, but that didn't slow her down. She showed no signs of giving in.

Mena gathered her courage and focused. "Enough," she said.

"Yes, that's enough, Reacher boy," Queen Veronica said. Her perfectly styled hair had started to fall out of place. "You should see you can't beat me. I'm more powerful than you'll ever be." She finally stood still so that she could stare at them condescendingly. Then she gasped. She looked as if she wanted to Travel but couldn't. "What have you done?"

Mena focused as Thomas had taught her. The flames blazed in a circle around Queen Veronica. Mena almost couldn't believe it had worked. She had actually done it, but she couldn't lose her concentration now. If she faltered, she would burn Queen Veronica, and she didn't want to hurt anyone, not even the mother who had abandoned her because she was believed to be Not Gifted.

"What is wrong with you?" Queen Veronica shrieked. "I know you want to kill me, but do you have to burn down the whole castle?"

"Please, Your Majesty," Thomas said calmly. "It's like we said. We want to help you."

Queen Veronica looked around frantically. "Leopold!" she screamed.

"I'm afraid we don't have much time," Thomas said. "We have to move. We'll borrow one of the royal cars; I can drive. Do you think you can hold that fire while we walk, Mena?"

"Yes," Mena said. It was easier to control the fire now, but she didn't dare break her focus. If she so much as blinked, there may be a disaster.

"You?" Queen Veronica said. She stared at Mena with shock and disgust. "You're doing this? I thought it was the Reacher boy. You're a useless servant girl."

"I think she has proven she is quite useful," Henry said. "Now walk."

** ** **

Zac squirmed and wiggled in King Leopold's arms as he tried to get free. Everywhere he looked there was nothing, just empty space. So this was what it looked like when you were Traveling and were between places. Zac didn't like it. It was scary. Zac also didn't like King Leopold. He knew he wasn't supposed to bite people, but he bit down on King Leopold's hand as hard as he could. He tasted salty blood.

"Stupid mutt!" King Leopold shouted. He threw Zac to the ground.

Even though it hurt, Zac was glad to hit the hard ground. It meant they had stopped Traveling.

Frankie! he yelled as loud as he could.

He looked around. He showed Frankie pictures of everything he saw. There was lots of grass with pretty wildflowers and stone walls. He knew this place! Mena had brought him here to do his business when he was still a secret. They hadn't Traveled far at all; they were just behind the castle.

Look, Frankie! This is where I am! Behind the castle!

Then something very frightening happened. There was a loud noise. It hurt Zac's ears. Something flew high over his head and almost hit King Leopold. When the little flying thing finally hit the ground, dirt sprayed everywhere. What was it? It wasn't a vase of flowers like that boy Henry threw. There were more flying things coming. If those little flying things could hurt the dirt so much, what would happen if one hit Zac? He needed to hide, but he was too scared to move. He tucked up and made himself as small as he could. All he really knew to do when there was danger was bark and bite, and he didn't think that would help him against whatever these things were.

Frankie! he cried. *I'm scared!*

I'm almost there, she said.

Then she really was there. She ran across the yard toward him. That gave him courage. He got up and ran to her. Then it happened. One of the things hit Frankie in the arm. She screamed, but she didn't stop. She scooped him up with her uninjured arm and ran back toward the castle.

"Dad, we have to get inside!" Frankie yelled. She didn't try to carry King Leopold like she did Zac.

"I don't believe it," King Leopold said. He kept moving around.

Maybe he was trying to avoid the scary things by Traveling the tiniest bits.

"Inside," Frankie repeated. She didn't slow down.

The kitchen door was closest, and that's where they went. When they got inside, Frankie fell to the floor, and Zac fell too. It hurt.

Sorry, Frankie said. *It hurts so much.* With her good arm, she stroked Zac's soft fur.

Zac was thankful. Frankie had saved him again. Surely, those things would have hurt him. Frankie was very hurt. Her arm was bleeding. It wasn't like the bite his puppy teeth had given King Leopold. The sleeve of her shirt was soaked in red.

What do we do, Frankie?

I don't know. It hurts.

She pet him as she cried. He cried too.

CHAPTER TWENTY-ONE

Frankie was cold and numb. Her energy was fading fast. Maybe she was going into shock. She pet Zac to keep herself busy. Otherwise, she could probably fall asleep right there on the kitchen floor. They hadn't had much of a plan about today, but she didn't think getting shot was part of it. Her father lumbered into the kitchen and locked the door behind him. He muttered to himself, completely oblivious to Frankie and Zac on the floor.

"My own guards shooting at me," he said.

Frankie remembered the "guard" outside her parents' quarters. Mark hadn't trusted her with too many details of the rebels' plan, but now she realized their plan was a pretty good one.

"They're not your guards," she whispered. "They're rebels. They probably hurt or killed your guards to steal their uniforms."

King Leopold regarded her. "We need to leave. Your mother and I will get you somewhere safe, get you to a doctor."

"No, I'm not leaving my friends. There's a doctor where we're going. You need to come with us too. It's not safe here – " Frankie stopped. Talking required too much energy. She clasped her arm. Frankie vaguely remembered something from science class about putting pressure on a wound. She tried to not think about all the blood; thinking about it would only make it worse.

"We were perfectly safe here until you showed up with your rebels," King Leopold said.

"Can't you see I'm not with them?" Frankie said. "If I was, would they have shot me?"

Her father didn't look like he believed her, but something else grabbed his attention. "Fire! The castle's on fire! They've lit the castle on fire!"

No, they didn't. Frankie thought she knew where the fire was coming from. "Mena! In here!" She tried to shout, but she was so weak that her voice was barely louder than a whisper.

I'll tell her, Zac said. He barked and barked.

Frankie saw her mother first. She looked like an angel surrounded by Mena's fire. The fire dropped when Mena saw Frankie. Frankie had made Mena lose her concentration. Mena rushed to Frankie and started to bandage her wound with kitchen towels.

"What happened?" Mena asked.

"Shot," Frankie said.

"David will fix you up properly, but this will have to do for now,"

Mena said as she secured the makeshift bandage.

Frankie's arm still throbbed, but at least now it couldn't bleed so much. She wondered if she would have a permanent scar.

"Look out! There's another one!" Henry said.

A "guard" stalked into the kitchen with a gun. He grinned like the scene before him was too good to be true. Frankie thought she recognized him as one of the rebels from the bakery meeting, but she wasn't sure.

"Look at this," the imposter guard said. "A family reunion. How touching." He raised his gun.

Zac barked at him. Mena threw a fireball at him. Henry threw a heavy frying pan at his head. Burned and unconscious, the imposter guard fell to the ground.

"You're actually pretty useful, Henry," Frankie said.

"And you look terrible," Henry said. "Come on. Let's get to the car."

Helen stormed into the kitchen. "What is all the commotion out here?" she demanded. She put her hand to her face when she saw the unconscious guard and the blood surrounding Frankie. Whatever she had expected to see in the kitchen, it wasn't this.

"We're under attack!" King Leopold said. He paced the kitchen nervously. "I can't believe it, but I'm leaving with this lot. At least they haven't tried to kill me yet."

Helen tugged at her apron anxiously. "What can I do?"

"Go to the fortress," Queen Veronica said. "It's protocol. I'm sure most of the servants are there already. The rebels won't bother you, even if they do find you. It's us they're after." If Queen Veronica was as nervous as the others, she didn't show it. She stood up tall and composed.

"Yes, Your Majesty," Helen said. She didn't have to be told twice. She hustled off.

"Everyone else, to the car," Queen Veronica said. She was used to being in charge. The others didn't mind her giving the orders. Frankie was relieved her parents finally understood that they needed to leave.

Frankie stood and weakly followed the crowd to the garage. Zac stuck next to her on one side, and Mena stuck to the other. They were met by Adam. If Frankie had enough energy, she would have groaned. She had hoped to never see him again.

"King Leopold, Queen Veronica! I was just coming to get you," Adam said. "Pardon me for being so bold, but are you or Joey in need of an armored van? I know you are Travelers, but these are dangerous times. Armored cars are safer than Traveling."

"Thank you, young man, but I can drive," Thomas said. "You stay here in the fortress with the servants. You will be safe there."

Adam opened the door of the van. "Let me take you. I know a safe place we can go."

Queen Veronica climbed into the van. "Stop arguing. Let the driver handle it."

"He probably is a better driver than me," Thomas said.

"No, don't trust him," Frankie whispered.

"What's the risk?" Henry said. "Maybe he can help us. If he tries anything, I think I've proven I can knock people out, and then Thomas can drive us."

"Fine," Frankie said. She thought they would be better off if they left Adam here, but she didn't want to waste what little energy she had by arguing with Henry.

"Excellent. Then let's hurry off," Thomas said. "We have what we came here for." He reached out a hand to help Frankie into the van.

"Wait!" Mena cried, causing everyone to freeze. "Queen Izabel said to bring a cameraman."

"What on earth would she want that for?" King Leopold said as he fastened his seatbelt. "Does she think we're going to go on television and address the kingdom in the middle of all this?"

"Beats me," Thomas said. "But she must have a reason. Do you have one handy?"

"There's a camera up in our quarters, but the cameramen will be in the fortress," King Leopold said. "It's too dangerous to go run all around the castle. Just forget it."

Frankie ducked as something whizzed by her head. It was much too large to be a bullet. What were those rebels up to now?

"Sorry," Henry said sheepishly.

Frankie looked up to see Henry holding the camera. "I know you like knocking people out, but don't knock me out."

Zac gave him a bark for good measure.

"Great, you have your camera, and I'm sure I can figure out how to work that thing," Adam said. "Let's go! The rest of you get in the van!"

"Wait!" Queen Veronica said.

Frankie sighed. What now? Yes, they had almost forgotten the camera, but they really should leave. It was only a matter of time until more rebels found them.

"Joey!" Queen Veronica said. "He's still up in his quarters. He won't know what's going on. We can't leave him."

Joey, the heir. Frankie still didn't know anything about him other than he was her replacement. She shouldn't like him, but she knew he was likely only a child. Her mother was right. They couldn't leave him in the castle by himself, especially not in the middle of an invasion. Someone had to get him, and if anyone knew the sneaky ways of getting up to those quarters, it was her.

"I'll go," she said.

"No!"

"You're already injured!"

"No!"

Everyone was talking at once, and it was making her head hurt.

Frankie, I'll go, Zac said. *You can show me where to go, and I'll bring him here.*

** ** **

King Leopold and Queen Veronica didn't like this idea, but Zac didn't care. He didn't like them. Apparently no one could leave unless this Joey was with them. Frankie was very brave and would go herself, but Zac couldn't let her put herself in danger. He had to be brave this time. He was smaller than Frankie, so if those scary things came again, he had a better chance of avoiding them than she did.

Good, keep going up those stairs. You're almost there, Frankie said.

Zac scampered up the stairs as quickly as he could. He didn't have much experience with stairs. It was hard! He would have to go down the stairs eventually. Would that be any easier? Finally, he reached the top.

Now go to the right, Frankie said.

Zac broke into a run.

No, that's left! The other way! Frankie said.

Zac turned around. *You never taught me right and left,* he said as he ran.

Sorry, it never came up. We'll have to work on it, Frankie said. *Stop! That's my door, or Joey's door. You have to go in there and get him.*

Zac pushed on the door, but it didn't budge. He couldn't reach the doorknob. How was he supposed to get in? He would have to get Joey to come out here. He wished he could talk to Joey like he talked to Frankie; that would make this a lot easier. Instead, he resorted to barking.

Oh, come on, Joey! Frankie thought. *Don't make him bark all day. We have to go!*

Zac quite agreed.

A boy opened the door. He was small, pale, and skinny. This must be Joey. Zac stopped barking.

"A puppy? What are you doing here?" the boy said. He reached down and pet Zac's head.

Now get him to follow you, Frankie said.

Zac started for the stairs. They had to get back to the others quickly. He peeked back to make sure Joey was keeping up. Joey wasn't following him at all. Hadn't anyone trained this boy? The human was supposed to walk next to the dog. Zac wished he still had the leash, but that had become detached at some point. He trotted back and grabbed the end of Joey's long sleeve with his teeth.

"Do you want me to come with you?" Joey said.

Yes! Zac wagged his tail.

"I don't think I'm supposed to leave, but I guess I can come play with you for a little bit," Joey said.

Something caught Zac's eye. They had to be quick, but this would only take a second, and it was for Foxy. He darted into the room and grabbed the teddy bear. The fuzzy fabric didn't smell like Frankie. The bear must belong to Joey. Hopefully, he wouldn't mind sharing. Holding the bear in his mouth, Zac led the boy into the hall.

Then there were scary things flying around. Joey dropped to the ground next to Zac. Oh no, was Joey hurt like Frankie? Zac looked him over. No, he wasn't hurt. It looked like he was using Zac's strategy of staying low to avoid the flying things. Maybe the boy was a little smart after all. There was a man coming down the hall. Zac recognized his clothes. This man was what the others called a guard, and Zac knew he was a bad man. They had to get down the stairs. Zac started to crawl.

Joey stood up tall. *No!* Zac thought as loudly as he could even though Joey couldn't hear him. *We have to get away!*

"What's going on?" Joey asked the man. His voice shook slightly.

"You must be one of them! Get him!" the man yelled. The man ran down the hall toward Joey and Zac. There were others behind him.

We're in trouble, Frankie. What do we do? Zac said.

Joey scooped Zac up and held him tight. "Stick with me, little guy," he said. Then they were Traveling. Zac didn't like Traveling any better this time, but it was over in seconds. They hit solid ground, and Joey set Zac down on the floor.

"Darn," Joey said. "I'm still not accurately hitting my destinations. I was trying to get us outside."

Zac looked around. He knew this place. They were in the kitchen again, and that meant the others weren't far away. He let go of the bear momentarily to give Joey's sleeve a tug. He sprinted for the garage with Joey close behind.

Almost there, Frankie! he said. He ran as fast as his paws would let him.

When they got to the garage, everyone was in the big van. They had left the door open, and Frankie was the lookout.

"We did it! Here they come!" Frankie said excitedly.

Zac leapt into Frankie's lap. Joey climbed into the van after him. Joey slammed the door shut before collapsing into a seat.

I knew we could do it, Frankie, Zac said.

Me too, Frankie said. *But did you really have to stop and get a teddy bear?*

** ** **

Frankie, hurry back! We need help! Foxy said. The people in the car were very hurt. Foxy learned their names were Queen Izabel, King Sean, and Paul. She had never met a king or queen before, but this king and queen seemed nice. She guessed Paul helped them and drove them around, but right now he was too hurt to do much of anything. Queen Izabel liked to pet Foxy's soft fur, so Foxy sat next to her. She liked to be petted. Petting was usually calming, but right now Foxy couldn't help being frightened. There were people outside of the car. They banged on the sides like they wanted to get in. Foxy knew if the people could get in, they would harm them. They would kick and punch and maybe even burn Foxy and these nice people. She tried to be brave, but it was hard. She called and called to Frankie for help.

Just stay in the car, Foxy. We're on our way, Frankie said. Frankie's voice sounded low and far away. That was strange. Usually Foxy could hear her loud and clear or not at all.

Without meaning to, Foxy let out a whimper. So much for being brave.

"Shh, it'll be okay, Foxy," David said. "This car has armor. That makes it very tough. No one can get us in here."

David was smart. If he said it would be okay, it must be true, but she was still scared. She wished these bad people would go away and leave them alone. She hid her face so that she wouldn't see the bad people out the window.

Foxy, we're here. Can you hear me?

Yes! Foxy said. Frankie still sounded strange, but Foxy could hear her.

We're going to get those people away from the car.

Okay. Foxy picked her head up and looked out the window. Rocks and fireballs flew through the air. Some hit the car but didn't seem to hurt it. David was right. This car was very tough. The bad people were not as tough. They ran down the street, away from the rocks and fire. Some of them caught on fire and screamed. Foxy knew where the fire was coming from – Mena. Mena was sweet, but she was also tough. She was helping to protect them.

When the bad people were gone, David opened the door. Thomas, Frankie, and Zac climbed in.

"We're going to follow the others. We're going somewhere safe," Thomas said. "I'll drive. Patch up Frankie if you can."

Frankie fell into the middle seat next to Queen Izabel. Half of her shirt was red with blood. She was very hurt. Foxy whimpered. She and Zac sat close to Frankie while David examined her arm.

"We need to clean out the wound and stitch you up," David said.

"There are medical supplies in the black bag over there," Queen Izabel said.

"Why on earth didn't you say so before?" David said.

"None of us needed it," Queen Izabel said. "There's nothing you can do for all these bruises and sore bodies except wait for them to heal. I'm no doctor, but I think Frankie needs more than that."

David found the necessary supplies. He put some kind of medicine on Frankie's arm. Foxy knew that it stung because Frankie told them so. Foxy snuggled closer to her. Then David started to sew Frankie back together. Foxy had never seen a person sewn up before, but it reminded her of the sewing she had seen Mena do, like the pretty pink collar Mena had made for her.

Zac set something in front of Foxy. It looked like the toy he always played with at home.

I hope you like that teddy bear, Foxy, Frankie said. *Zac stole it just for you.*

CHAPTER TWENTY-TWO

When they arrived at the safe place, a flustered-looking man and woman fussed over them and wanted to take care of them. It had been a long day, and Frankie was tired. She just wanted to sit. She sat at a table between Mena and Joey. The dogs had made themselves comfortable on the floor under the table. Zac napped with his head on Frankie's foot. Frankie would like a nap too, but apparently there was about to be some sort of television address. She wasn't sure who was organizing the address, whether it was her parents or King Sean and Queen Izabel. She was too tired to ask questions.

"Where are we anyway?" she said. Maybe she was almost too tired to ask questions.

"I've been here before," Mena said. "I thought it was a restaurant."

Frankie looked around. Now that she thought about it, this place did look like a restaurant. There were lots of tables with fancy tablecloths.

"It is a restaurant," Adam said. He sat on Joey's other side. "It is also my parents' house. Don't worry. We're safe here. My parents don't want anything to do with the rebels." That explained who the flustered man and woman were.

Frankie didn't like Adam, but if he had gotten them to a safe place, maybe he wasn't all bad. Frankie wondered about the reason for the change of heart. Maybe he still liked Mena and was trying to impress her. Frankie heard boys could be tricky like that. She should warn Mena. Then again, Mena could set people on fire. Mena could take care of herself.

"Are you ready, cameraman?" Queen Izabel called.

Both kings and queens were seated at a long table. David had recommended King Sean sit for the address due to his sprained knee, so they had decided that both kings and queens would sit. Queen Veronica fussed with her hair in an effort to look perfect for the camera.

Adam stood and took up his post with the camera. He pushed a few buttons, and a red light came on. This address would be shown live all over Superion. Frankie took a deep breath. Even though she wasn't required to go on screen for this address, she was still nervous. This address would either result in peace or more fighting. She strongly hoped it was the former.

"Hello," Queen Izabel said. She smiled pleasantly despite her bruised face. "My name is Queen Izabel, and this is my husband, King Sean. We are the elected rulers of Allton. Many years ago, Superion was part of Allton. Superion was made its own unique kingdom as an experiment. At first, Superion was very similar to Allton. Then Allton introduced a variable. Random people of Superion were injected with a virus. The virus didn't have immediate effects, but in the next generation, some people did show signs of the virus. The virus manifested itself in several different ways. You would call these manifestations Gifts. Some people could Travel. Some people could read minds, and others could move objects without even having to touch them. Still others remained free of the virus; you would call them Not Gifted. Please note that those with the virus, the Gifted, are not ill; they are just different."

Queen Izabel paused to take a sip of water. Frankie's eyes were wide. How had they never learned about this in school? She spotted Adam's parents watching the address from the side of the room. They looked shocked as well. This history lesson must be a surprise to everyone.

"As you can imagine, it has been incredibly interesting for Allton to observe how Gifts impact a society," Queen Izabel said. "It is my belief that the Gifts were intended to make Superion a stronger society, that those with Gifts would use them for the good of all. Unfortunately, that has not been the case. The Gifts have divided you. Look at the differences in finances and lifestyle, all because one has a virus that the other does not. When this rebellion began, we knew it was time for our kingdom to intervene. After all, we're the ones who started all this."

"What are you trying to say?" King Leopold cut in. "Did you come here to fix us, to take away our Gifts?"

Queen Izabel shook her head. "No, we do not want to do that. The Gifts are part of you now."

"We believe it is possible to keep your Gifts intact while also having a just and equal society," King Sean said. "That begins with a change in leadership."

"What's wrong with my leadership?" King Leopold demanded. He pounded his fist on the table angrily. "The throne has been in my family for generations."

"That is exactly the problem," King Sean said calmly. "With the throne passing from one generation of your family to the next, that gives the citizens of Superion no say in the matter. We propose that Superion go back to having an elected king and/or queen with an election every ten years. The next election will be in two weeks' time. Citizens may nominate themselves or someone else. You are welcome to nominate yourselves, King Leopold, Queen Veronica."

"We will go along with this silly show of an election, fine," King Leopold said. "That is what will make you and the rebels happy and stop all this nonsense, but you and the rebels are just a small group. You will see. Queen Veronica and I will win the election. We have proven what good leaders we are. If anyone doesn't like us, I would encourage them to vote for our daughter, Frances. She has a Gift no one has seen before."

Frankie hid her face in her hands. Why was she being dragged into this? A short time ago, her parents had disowned her. Now her father would want her to be a queen to keep the family in power.

"For those looking for a bit of a change, I would also like to suggest our heir, Joey," Queen Veronica said. "He is a Traveler. As my husband and I have shown, Travelers make excellent leaders."

"Yes well, thank you for the endorsements," Queen Izabel said hastily.

Frankie didn't think that had been part of the plan.

"Superion, you started out as an experiment, but you turned into a good and Gifted kingdom," Queen Izabel said. "After so much division, show us that you can be a good and equal kingdom once again."

"Thank you," Frankie said as a plate of pasta was placed in front of her. Her stomach growled. She was starving. It seemed like ages ago they had been foraging in the castle pantry. Had it really only been this morning? She gazed down the long table. Except for some scrapes and scares, her friends had made it through this day unharmed. She had been the bloodiest by far, but David had assured her that she would make a full recovery. Even Queen Izabel, King Sean, and their assistant were going to be okay. Frankie couldn't believe her parents were able to sit so peacefully with Queen Izabel and King Sean. Being royalty had been their lives, and now it looked like only a short time before the king and queen titles were taken away. Then again, they were being delusional about the whole situation. They expected to win the election, but Frankie couldn't see that happening with the way they hated the Not Gifted.

Frankie ate her pasta quietly. The others chatted pleasantly around her, but she was too tired to talk. Zac hit her ankles with his paws.

Can I share some of your dinner, Frankie? I'm so hungry!

Frankie supposed all dogs begged, but they got to be a little bit louder about it if you happened to be an Animal Minder. She also knew very well that Zac had eaten his own dinner. Adam's mother had kindly made sure that Zac and Foxy were fed. Frankie snuck Zac a few bites of pasta under the table anyway.

"Why are you feeding that horrid dog?" King Leopold said.

"He's hungry," Frankie said.

"I like him," Joey piped up. The boy had barely said a word all day.

"Well, I don't," King Leopold said. He held up his bitten hand to display his wound. It looked pathetic compared to Frankie's gunshot wound.

"I like him because he helped me," Joey said. "He warned me that the bad people were coming. He's really smart, and he's cute."

Zac wagged his tail. *Smart and cute. Am I really smart and cute, Frankie?*

Yes, you are. Frankie snuck him a bite of bread.

"I don't believe all that," King Leopold said. "He's a dumb animal. It was sheer luck that you got out of the castle."

"That's not true, and you know it," Thomas said sternly. "Animals are intelligent, and Frankie is able to communicate with them. You like that your daughter has a Gift when it suits you, but you don't like what her Gift is because of your prejudice against animals. It's foolish just like your prejudice against the Not Gifted."

King Leopold let out a snort of disbelief. He looked like he wanted to give Thomas some horrible punishment, like years of hard labor.

Frankie, tell your dad it's okay that he doesn't like me. I don't like him either, Zac said.

Frankie repeated as she was told.

"He can't say anything. He's a stupid dog," King Leopold said. "You're making that all up."

"We hear each other, whether you want to believe it or not," Frankie said. "That's how I told him to find Joey. Why do you hate animals so much anyway?"

"Because a dog attacked my great-great-great-grandfather," King

Leopold said. "No dog is to be trusted. No animal is to be trusted."

"The family has been strongly opposed to animals ever since," Queen Veronica said. "We don't like to talk about King Leo and his ordeal. He was a good man, and a dog bit him. It was a black dog, like that one you run around with."

"King Leo died years and years ago," Frankie said. "How do you know he was a good man? How do you even know what happened? He could have provoked the dog."

"Dogs are evil," was all King Leopold had to say.

Frankie thought it ridiculous that her parents were anti-animal all because of something that may or may not have happened generations ago. Then again, they had also sent their daughters away for being supposedly Not Gifted. She guessed she would never see eye to eye with her parents.

Adam's parents set desserts and drinks on the table. Frankie gladly took a piece of cake and a mug of cocoa. She never turned down dessert, and it had been forever since she had hot cocoa.

Please save me some cake! Zac said.

Frankie turned to Joey between bites of cake. "How did you get to be the heir anyway? Are we related?"

Joey jumped and stared at Frankie with big eyes. He was so startled at being addressed that he almost knocked his cocoa over, but Mena saved it from making too much of a mess.

"It's okay," Frankie said. "I'm just curious."

"You're not related," Queen Veronica said for him. "Joey was predicted to be a powerful Traveler. We've had our eye on him for years in case you didn't work out."

"I'm not supposed to Travel," Joey said. "I haven't been trained yet. I'm only eleven, so I'm not old enough to take the Test. I guess there's no more castle for me. It will be back to my family."

"That's not such a bad thing," Mena said kindly. "You will have plenty of time to Travel and work when you're older. For now, you can be a kid, go to school, play."

Joey didn't look cheered by this. Zac gave his hand a lick, and that did seem to cheer him. Zac and Joey had helped each other today; they were friends. Plus, Zac was hoping for some of Joey's cake.

Hey Frankie, I have an idea, Foxy said.

What's that? Frankie said.

Queen Izabel likes me. Maybe I can get Queen Veronica to like me too, to show her that dogs are nice.

Queen Izabel and Queen Veronica are two very different people, but you can try to make friends if you want to. I guess you have a slightly better chance than Zac. They seem to really hate black dogs.

Foxy licked Queen Veronica's sandaled feet under the table. It made Queen Veronica laugh.

"What's so funny?" King Leopold demanded.

"It tickles," Queen Veronica said.

Foxy put her blonde head in Queen Veronica's lap and looked up at her with big brown eyes.

"Travel away! It looks ready to attack!" King Leopold shouted.

Queen Veronica looked down at Foxy with a very puzzled expression. "I don't know. She doesn't look mean. She looks...sweet. Maybe these dogs are nice. The black one did go get Joey." Queen Veronica hesitantly pat Foxy on the head.

See, it's working! Foxy said as she nuzzled closer to Queen Veronica.

I think I'm better off over here, Zac said from next to Joey. *This one is sharing his dessert. Nice kid. Actually Frankie, I have to go potty.*

Yes, so do I! Foxy said.

Frankie yawned. It had been a very long day. "I have to put the dogs out," she announced as she stood up.

"I'll take them," Mena offered. "You look exhausted."

** ** **

Mena held the leashes in her right hand. Zac's leash had gotten lost in their adventure, so Adam's mother had lent them some rope to use as a temporary leash. Adam's parents had been very kind to take care of them, especially without notice.

"Don't go too far, guys. It's really dark out here."

She should have brought a flashlight, but she hadn't thought of it. She was as tired as the rest of them, and her brain wasn't working properly. No, her brain really wasn't working properly; she of all people didn't need to stumble around in the dark. She held out her left hand and focused. Within moments, a fireball hovered over her palm. It was tiny, but it was bright. It didn't burn her; it just illuminated the yard.

Mena was relieved to see only grass and flowers. There were no hidden dangers lurking out here.

"Mena?"

Mena jumped, and the dogs barked. With her loss of concentration, her fireball blinked out. She lit another one before she turned around. She was face to face with Adam. This was his parents' house; she shouldn't be surprised to see him.

"Sorry," Adam said. "I guess I should know better than to sneak up on you. You could burn me to a crisp."

Zac barked. Mena didn't blame him, but she shushed him anyway.

"He still doesn't like me, does he?" Adam said.

"You would have to ask Frankie. She's the translator, but no, I don't think he does," Mena said. "Can you blame him? You're the one who wanted us kicked out of the castle."

Adam shoved his hands in his pockets. "I did the right thing. The king and queen didn't want animals there." He was entirely unapologetic.

"There's nothing wrong with a young girl having a dog," Mena said. She stared at her fireball as she spoke. It spun in circles over her palm.

"Why should I care what a silly princess wants? That's not my responsibility. My loyalty is to the king and queen."

Mena's fireball continued to spin. "What about today? You helped us."

"My only concern was for the king and queen, not the rest of you, but taking you all to safety seemed like the only option. With your rebellious good intentions, you and your friends probably would have gotten the king and queen killed."

"So that's all you care about, your loyalty to the king and queen? What about you? Don't you ever think about what is right and wrong?"

"I am a citizen of Superion. I trust my king and queen," Adam said.

Mena knew not all Not Gifted were rebels. She had certainly been hesitant about the rebels herself, but was blind loyalty to the royals a good thing? Shouldn't people think for themselves?

"Anyway, that's not why I came out here," he said. "I'm sorry about how things worked out between us. I wish you hadn't gone away with the princess. If you're staying in the city this time, would you like to go on another date with me?"

Maybe she was a little delirious from being so tired, but Mena had to keep herself from laughing. "No, I don't think that's a good idea," she managed to say with a straight face.

Her recent adventures had changed her. A few weeks ago, she never would have thought of turning down a date. A servant girl from the country didn't get asked on many dates. Now she was starting to see the world in a new way. Society didn't have to be as divided as she had always thought, and there was someone she liked very much. David may be Gifted and a doctor, but she didn't have to look at him like he was leagues above her anymore.

EPILOGUE

Frankie sat on the sofa next to Mena. Zac and Foxy were cuddled up at their feet. They were once again gathered in Thomas' living room. The latest installment of mandatory viewing was about to start.

"It's healing well," David said as he re-bandaged her arm. "How does it feel?"

"Okay," Frankie said.

There had been offers for her to stay in the city. Adam's parents had offered her a room, or she could have stayed with her own parents. She had turned them all down. The quiet of the country had been more appealing. It wasn't like she could do much with her injured arm, and she could heal just as well in the country as she could in the city. She liked the company here, and she had worked some. She had helped Betty mind the sheep.

"Who do you think it will be?" Thomas said.

Frankie shrugged. She was so nervous. She was always nervous for one reason or another when it came to mandatory viewing.

"It's exciting. I wonder who it will be," Mena said. She nudged Frankie's good arm.

Frankie knew there was a decent chance she would be named queen. An exaggerated story of how she had gotten her parents out of the castle and away from the rebels who wanted to hurt them had been all over the news. The reporters talked and talked about how she was supportive of the Not Gifted, but she was Gifted herself so must like the Gifted too. Frankie was glad Mena's parents didn't have a television. She had been able to avoid much of the gossip.

She had heard of some of the other favorites. Mark was a favorite among the rebels, and he wanted to be king. Even in this quiet country town, Frankie couldn't go anywhere without seeing Mark's posters and banners, campaigning for votes. King Leopold and Queen Veronica expected to stay king and queen, but according to Thomas and all the reporters, that was highly unlikely. Then there were the local celebrities, people expected to get lots of votes in their own local communities but unknown elsewhere in the kingdom. Frankie hoped one of the local celebrities would get enough votes to be named king or queen.

"You may be going back to the castle, Zac," David said.

They had really good food there, Zac told Frankie.

"I hope it's not me. I have no idea how to run a kingdom," Frankie said, finally voicing her anxiety out loud.

"No one person knows how to run a whole kingdom. That's why royals hire advisors," Thomas said.

At last, Queen Izabel and King Sean appeared on the screen. Their bruises had faded, and they looked much better than they had two weeks ago. Frankie barely heard their speech about this being a new beginning for Superion. She was too busy staring at the envelope in Queen Izabel's hand.

"It is an honor to announce..." Queen Izabel said.

Mena clutched Frankie's hand tightly.

"The new ruler of Superion is Frances Westwood. Congratulations, Queen Frances."

Mena, Thomas, and David broke into cheers. Not wanting to be left out of the excitement, Zac and Foxy jumped up and wagged their tails. Zac even threw his teddy bear onto Frankie's lap. Frankie felt numb.

"I'm glad you're so happy," Frankie said when she found her voice. "You're my first three advisors."

"Are you sure?" Mena said. "You should take some time to think about this."

Frankie nodded. "I'm positive. I'm gifted to have all of you in my life, and I'm going to need your help if I'm going to make a decent queen. What about you, Zac? Foxy? I could use your help too. Do you want to come to the castle and be my advisors?"

Yes! Foxy said.

Yes! Especially if there's cake and milk! Zac said.

ABOUT THE AUTHOR

Danielle loves books and dogs. When she's not writing, she can often be found adventuring with Heidi VI.

Made in the USA
Middletown, DE
27 August 2017